CW00739897

PLEASING THE PUNTERS

PLEASING THE PUNTERS

Dave Royle

THIRD HOUSE (PUBLISHERS)

First published May 1990 by Third House,
69 Regent Street, Exeter, Devon EX2 9EG

World Copyright © Dave Royle 1990

ISBN 1 870188 13 6

Photoset by Rapid Communications, Bristol BS3

Printed and bound by Bookplan, Worcester

For
Jo Reid and Tom Milward

Hat Trick

Jon stood on the top step. Helen held on to the door-frame and leaned forward to kiss him on the cheek. Frankie was sitting cross-legged on the living-room carpet, rolling a cigarette. Patches of light from the television flickered across his face.

'Night night, sweetheart,' Helen said.

'Take care,' Jon said. 'You go to bed. There's nothing we can do.'

'I'm going,' Helen said. She sniffed the cool air.

'You don't mean it about the baby, do you?'

'No, of course not,' Helen said. 'But half-way through the evening, I just wondered what we're doing. It seemed crazy. What's going to be *left*, for Christ's sake?' She rubbed her stomach absent-mindedly.

'Night, Frankie.'

'Night, babes. You run straight home, now.'

'Yessir.'

Frankie looked up and grinned at his brother.

'See you Saturday. . .'

'It's started raining,' Helen said, holding out her hand. 'You'll get wet.'

'Don't worry,' Jon said. 'I've got my new hat!' He pulled a black woolly hat from the left pocket of his jacket and pulled it down over his head.

'Christ, you really do look dangerous now,' Helen said, laughing. 'I still don't understand about all this.' She looked down at his jeans, rolled up to the top of his DMs. 'You say it's all to do with sex?'

'More or less,' Jon said, kicking the step twice with the heel of his boot.

1

'Christ, it must have been such fun for you lot.'

'The hat's great. Listen, if that baby goes without bootees because you've been too busy knitting me hats and pullovers, don't blame me.'

'I won't,' Helen said. 'Anyway, I had the wool spare. I told you – I was just seeing if I still remembered how to knit before I started anything proper.'

'Sleep tight. Keep the *Guardian* wall-chart safe for next time.'

'I suppose there *will* be a next time. . ?' Helen laughed and blew him a kiss. The sound of the knocker reverberated along the quiet street when she closed the door. Just as he turned onto the pavement, Jon heard a scraping noise behind him. It was Frankie, unfastening the window.

'What have I forgotten this time?'

'Nothing,' Frankie said, peering through a small gap above the window-sill. 'The Tories just took Ipswich.'

'Where's Ipswich?'

'Even Ipswich.'

'And Battersea!' Helen shouted from the room. 'Fucking Battersea!'

'Sorry kid,' Frankie said, with a lopsided smile. 'Looks like we're surrounded.'

It was quiet along the main road – almost deserted except for the occasional lorry carrying bags of vegetables from Covent Garden. There were a few people hurrying along the pavements, but otherwise Jon was alone. He passed the darkened shop windows, his reflection rippling against displays of clothes and shoes and empty food trays. It was a different street from the one he always saw choked with traffic. Now the air smelled almost fresh.

The rain fell in a fine mist for a minute or two and then died away. A police siren wailed, somewhere on the North Peckham Estate. Jon's feet crunched through broken glass on the pavement. He began to see things he'd never noticed before: the new estate agent's where the second-hand television shop had been; the faded sign painted on the brickwork high up on the side of the *Moulin*

2

Rouge Cocktail Bar; the black Venetian blinds and ruched curtains that were gradually replacing the yellowed nets in the windows above the shops.

Next to the greengrocer's, by the bus stop, someone had scrawled "Cape means South African" in blue felt-tip. Underneath, someone had sprayed "And Nigger = AIDS". The glass in the bus timetable board had been recently smashed. The timetables, soaked by the fine rain, hung in limp tatters, but the words on the wall seemed burned into the crumbling brickwork.

Someone was walking towards him. The figure got nearer and Jon saw it was Jimmy from downstairs.

'Hello Jon!'

'Hello Jimbo. Where've you been?'

'Up the Market.'

A car approached from the direction of the Oval. As it passed them, the driver blew his horn and flashed his lights. Hands waved from every window.

'I'm glad someone's 'appy,' Jimmy said. 'I watched the first hour and 'ad to go out.' He laughed. 'Only they 'ad it on the TV at the Market. Every miserable soddin' minute of it.'

'I've been up to my brother's,' Jon said. 'We just got pissed. Even Helen got pissed – and she's six months.'

'What else can you do?' Jimmy said, ' 'cept get pissed? I've 'ad a skinful. D'ya wanna come in for some tea?'

Jon hesitated. 'No, I think I'll stay out for a bit. I need the fresh air.'

'All right, but I'll be up a few hours if you change yer mind.'

'Cheers.' Jon looked up the road. 'Why is it so quiet?'

'No one's got any energy left,' Jimmy said. 'Everyone's well knackered already. Nothing left, you see. . .'

He patted Jon on the shoulder then ambled off towards the estate, his hands deep in his pockets, shoulders hunched as if against a cold wind.

Two cars roared across the traffic lights at the Green and swerved into the forecourt of the all-night garage. A girl got out of the front passenger seat of the first car. Jon was just passing the snooker club on the other side of the road. He slowed down and watched the girl. Her long fair hair hung in dishevelled curls around her bare shoulders. She was wearing a deep blue, full-length ball dress. The fabric sparkled like steel as she stood by the open car door under the forecourt lights, swaying slightly and frowning. The driver must have said something to her because she peered into the car and giggled loudly. The attendant in the cashier's booth watched them with vague amusement.

A motor cycle drew into the forecourt; and as it swept off the road, its headlight momentarily illuminated the sole occupant of the second car. Jon stopped walking altogether and leaned against the snooker club wall. The motor cyclist got off his bike and strode across to the booth. The girl giggled again and pulled a small bag from the car dashboard.

'Twenty?' she asked the driver. There seemed to be some confusion. 'No. Twenty? Yeah, but you want *twenty*? Does he?' She looked across at the second car.

'You want twenty Dunhill, Alec?' The blond boy in the second car must have nodded or said something to the girl, because she raised her hand and giggled again. Then she tottered across the forecourt to the booth, high heels scraping over the concrete.

Jon searched in his pocket and found two pound coins. He pushed himself away from the wall and ambled across the empty street towards the petrol pumps.

The motor cyclist was standing in front of the serving hatch, putting something in his pocket.

'Look, I'm really sorry,' the girl said, irritably, 'but we're late for a party. Can you hurry up?'

The man looked her up and down. As he moved off, he said: 'You won't be late for the party. Looks like it's only just started for *you*.' He zipped up his jacket and walked back to his bike, leaving the girl staring at him, open-mouthed.

Jon was just passing the second car when he heard the motor cyclist talk to the girl. He might have smiled if his attention hadn't been diverted by a broad wink from the blond boy in the driver's seat. He arched his eyebrows and strode off across the forecourt.

The girl gave the attendant a twenty-pound note.

'No, I'm really sorry,' she said, with a cursory glance into her bag, 'but I've only got twenties. Don't say you can't change it.'

The attendant mouthed something inaudible behind the plastic screen and opened the till. Jon heard a car door slam behind him. He looked round to see the blond boy lurching towards the booth. He was wearing a dinner jacket with a crooked black bow tie.

'What are you *doing*, Alec?' The girl's voice echoed around the garage forecourt. The motor cyclist roared off into the night, flicking a neat v-sign towards the booth as he passed by on the road.

'I wanted to get some air,' the boy said. Then he stared at Jon. 'And I wanted to see the view.'

The girl giggled. '*Honestly!*' she said.

The boy was having difficulty standing in one spot and looking at Jon at the same time.

'D'you wanna come to a party in Battersea?' he asked, smiling like a silly child.

'Victory party, is it?' Jon asked.

'Yes it is, actually,' the girl replied. She was watching the attendant. 'Can you *hurry*, please? Surely it can't be that difficult to find fifteen pounds in your till.'

The attendant mouthed something else and scowled through the partition. The girl pouted and crossed her arms.

'I'm not in a very celebratory mood, thanks,' Jon said.

The girl grabbed her change and looked disagreeably at the two men.

'Oh, *come on*, Alec. This area's giving me the creeps.'

'How about inviting me back to your place, then?' the boy said.

5

'You'll miss your party,' Jon said.

'Fuck the party.'

The girl was getting impatient.

'Look, Stewart wants to get going! Come *on*!'

'So do I,' the boy said. 'Let's have my cigarettes and I'll see you there later.'

The girl looked Jon up and down dubiously.

'Are you sure?' she said.

'Well?' the boy asked. 'Can I come back for coffee?'

'Why not?' Jon said.

'I'm Alec.'

'Hello Alec.'

The attendant shook his head slowly and looked at Jon through the screen with a weary smile. The girl flounced back to the car.

'Well, don't say I didn't warn you,' she called across the car park.

'Thanks!' Jon shouted.

'See you later!' Alec waved a loose arm at her.

The car swept past them and roared off up the road.

'She's got her nice dress caught in the door,' Jon said.

'She's a silly bitch,' Alec replied. He glowered at Jon, 'I'm really horny,' he said. 'I hope you are.'

'I live two streets away,' Jon said. 'Either you can leave the car here – if he lets you – or I'll walk and you can follow on.'

'We'll drive. Jump in.'

'You're pissed,' Jon said. 'I'm not driving anywhere with you.'

Alec reeled back against the car door.

'OK, you're the boss,' he said. 'I'm all yours.'

'I'll walk. You follow in the car.'

Jon stood at the bottom of the communal staircase and watched the boy park the car. First he drove over a bottle, which exploded with a loud pop, sending glass spraying across the path; then he backed into a metal bollard.

'Am I all right?' he asked.

'Terrific.'

Alec turned off the ignition and stumbled out of the car. He stood swaying on the spot for a few moments, squinting up at the block of flats. Lights were still on in a few windows. The sky was streaked with lines of deep blue above the rooftops.

It was the time of year when night turned to day in five minutes. Jon hurried upstairs. He didn't want anyone to see him with Alec.

'Come on. It's the second floor.'

As they passed the first floor landing, Jon noticed that Jimmy's kitchen light was on. He wished they had walked home together. Alec was taking the stairs slowly, watching each step.

'Christ!' he said. 'Look at all this shit. Don't you get tired of it? I mean, don't you get *sick* of all this shit?'

Jon shrugged his shoulders. 'Don't notice it after a while.'

'D'you live alone, then?'

'Yeah.'

'Got your own place, then?'

'Yeah.' Jon laughed through his nose. That was obvious, wasn't it, from his last answer? He felt Alec's hand touch his arse.

'I'm into skins.'

'I'm not a skin,' Jon said.

'You're dressed like one.'

'Doesn't make me a skin.'

'But you've got your hair cropped. I can see under that hat. And you've got your DMs on!' He started to giggle as they reached the second floor landing.

'I like being dominated.' His voice echoed along the deserted walkway. Jon fumbled in his pocket for the keys. A drainpipe outside the next flat started to spew out soapy water into a drain. The water frothed and bubbled, spilling onto the walkway. Jon tutted and turned the key.

'Fuckin' council,' he said. 'They were supposed to unblock the drains months ago.'

'I suppose you're Labour here,' Alec said.

'We're all Labour round here,' Jon said, opening the door.

Alec stood in the middle of the living room and looked around at the bookcases and piles of magazines.

'You've been having me on!' he said, giggling again.

'You what?' Jon was in the kitchen filling the kettle.

'Like reading, do you?'

Jon hurried into the living room. 'Can you keep your voice down? Most people'll be asleep.'

'Oh, sorry,' Alec whispered, sticking a nicotine-stained finger over his mouth.

'Milk and sugar?'

'Forget the coffee. Let's get on with it.'

'You what?'

Alec pawed at the front of Jon's jeans. Out of the corner of his eye, Jon saw the sky lightening through a crack in the curtains. It seemed very late.

'Sit down,' he said. 'I'll get some coffee. You could do with some.'

'Don't worry about me,' Alec said, leering across the room. 'I've been as horny as fuck for hours.'

'Well done,' Jon said. 'I'll get the coffee. D'you want milk and sugar?'

As soon as Jon put the mugs down on the table, Alec's hands reached across from the sofa.

'All right, Jon?' He tugged at the buttons on Jon's jeans. Jon closed his eyes. The long night had caught up with him. All he wanted to do was sleep. He hadn't needed any cigarettes. He'd deliberately gone over to the garage. Maybe it was time to grow up. . .

He opened his eyes. There was a large bulge in the front of Alec's trousers.

'Have you got any mates who could come over?'

Jon thought about Jimmy. He'd be lying in bed, probably, with a big mug of tea, watching the last results splutter out from concrete town halls and sports centres in dreary dormitory towns.

'Yeah, I've got mates,' he said. 'But they'll all be asleep now.'

Alec had pulled open the zip of his smart black trousers and was playing with his cock. It was big and banana-shaped, soft and chewable-looking. The tip glistened in the light from the table lamp. Jon was tempted for a moment.

'Let's see yours, then. I wanna see yours.'

'You want lots of things, don't you?' Jon said.

' 's what I've come back for, isn't it?' Alec pulled his cock from his trousers. 'Let's see yours.'

Jon started to unbutton his flies. Alec lay sprawled on the sofa, staring with his mouth open. When he glimpsed flesh under Jon's boxer shorts, he sat up.

'Give it to me!'

'How much have you had to drink?' Jon asked.

'Dunno.'

'How much? Where were you earlier?'

'At Smith Square first. Then at a party in Blackheath.'

'You *are* a busy boy,' Jon said. 'And next you're off to Battersea, to celebrate another Tory scalp.'

'What you on about?'

'You stink of alcohol!' Jon said. 'You're disgusting! You make me feel sick.'

'Oh yeah, get rough!' Alec was crawling around the carpet on his knees. 'Go on, treat me like shit!'

'You *are* shit.'

'Yeah! Yeah! Talk dirty! Take control.' Alec started to masturbate. His face had turned bright red.

'Got any poppers?'

'You like them, do you?'

'Yeah!'

'No, I haven't got any. You slimy Tory bastard!'

Alec pushed his face forward and bit Jon's thigh. Jon recoiled.

'You bastard! Watch your fucking teeth!'

'D'you like girls? Shall I fetch Kate from the party and bring her back here? Wanna watch me shaft her? Oh, fuck, I'm coming!'

'Not on my bloody carpet, you're not! Not on my. . .'

'Oh, fuck!'

Jon didn't say anything. He stood back against the table and buttoned up his jeans. Alec was still kneeling on the floor, swaying from side to side, the tip of one shirt tail soaking up semen from the carpet.

'It's a hired suit. . .'

Jon closed his eyes.

'I've come,' Alec explained, pointing to the carpet and looking up at Jon.

'I noticed.'

'I ought to go to the party. Gotta go.'

'Yeah, your friends'll be worried. They'll think something's happened to you.'

Alec smiled lazily.

'I knew I was safe with you,' he said. 'I wasn't fooled by you. I knew you weren't *really* a skinhead.'

'Oh yeah.'

'Yeah!' He staggered to his feet. 'I mean, look at all these books.'

'Clever boy.'

Alec pushed his limp cock back inside his trousers and did up the zip. He left his shirt tails hanging damp round his thighs.

'His majority was 857,' he said.

'Whose?'

'The Tory at Battersea.'

'Oh, yeah?'

'We'll do better next time. We won't stop now.'

Jon laughed. 'Christ, you and your friends must think Christmas has come six months early.' He felt envious.

Alec was inspecting a white stain on the left leg of his trousers.

'They're hired. . .'

'Time to go,' Jon said, guiding him towards the hall. 'Are you always such a selfish bastard?'

'Eh?' Alec struggled into his jacket and found his keys.

'Not just a fascist, but a sexual fascist too, eh?'

A frown crossed Alec's pretty, bloated face.

10

'Fancied a bit of rough, didn't you? Didn't care about anything but getting what *you* wanted.'

'Don't get nasty with me,' Alec said, sounding almost sober. 'I could call the police.'

'Bollocks, pipsqueak, you wouldn't dare,' Jon said, pressing his face very close against Alec's. He could still smell the stale alcohol on the boy's breath.

'Stained many skinheads' carpets, have you?'

'But you're not a skinhead. . .'

'What if I am or not?'

'I'm going,' Alec said, edging towards the door.

'You're going, all right,' Jon said. 'If you're still out for a raunchy time, take the lift down. You can get off on the smell of piss. And if you *really* want some rough treatment. . .'

Jon lunged his right fist into Alec's stomach. The boy's skin collapsed like a soft cushion. He crumpled up, choking and gasping for breath.

'Now fuck off, you bastard, and join your Gestapo friends in Battersea.' Jon opened the door. The sky was dark turquoise and flecked with strands of grey cloud. Everything looked very sharp and clean. He pushed the heaving body out onto the walkway.

'Go on, fuck off. I'm not going in till I've watched you drive off. You got just what you asked for.'

Alec grimaced up at him with small, frightened eyes. He was still bent almost double, clutching his stomach. Jon was surprised at how calm he felt. He hadn't hit anyone since junior school.

He watched Alec stagger off towards the stairs; then he waited until he'd heard the dragging footsteps reach the ground, and the metallic sound of the car door being unlocked and opened. There was a moment of silence after the door was slammed shut; then the ignition was switched on. Jon didn't look over the balcony: he kept his eyes fixed on the marbled sky and the outline of the concrete tower-block way in the distance. He heard the car drive off, out of the estate and through the empty streets towards the garage. He traced the movement of the

11

car until it faded away on the road towards Brixton, leaving behind the sound of birds waking in the scrubby trees.

He sponged the stained area on the carpet and glanced at his watch. It was four thirty. He picked up his keys and went back out onto the walkway, closing and locking the door behind him. Then he went down to the first floor. Jimmy's kitchen light was on. He tapped lightly on the door and called through the letter-box:

'Jimmy, it's me.'

Jimmy was in boxer shorts and a grubby white t-shirt. He had dark rings under his eyes. Further on, in the living room, voices were talking on the television.

' 'ello, Jon.'

'Hello, Jimbo. Is the tea still on?'

Jimmy smiled. 'Yeah, come in.'

'I picked someone up after I saw you.'

'Fuck me! You work fast!' Jimmy padded into the kitchen. 'So did 'e cheer you up?'

'No,' Jon said. 'He made me feel worse.'

'We need a good kip. Sleep here with me, eh?'

'Yeah. Thanks.'

They went into the bedroom. Jimmy had been lying in bed watching the television. The duvet was in a crumpled heap and there was a sandwich on a plate with a Jimmy-sized bite out of one corner. The room smelled stale and comforting.

'Look!' Jimmy pointed to the TV. 'There's the bit outside Tory H.Q. again. Look at them!' He sounded like he was about to cry.

They stood in the middle of the room and put their arms round each other.

'Like the new 'at!' Jimmy said, breathing into Jon's ear.

Jon stroked Jimmy's hair. It felt like velvet. A voice on the television rose above the cheering:

'We must do something about those inner cities.'

Pleasing the Punters

Down in the underground at Piccadilly Circus, a man in gamekeeper's knickerbockers and a tweed jacket is playing a harp. People are throwing coins into an upturned cap at his feet: against the wall, a ghetto blaster is playing flamenco music. Michael is in a hurry, but he slows down and observes the man for a few moments. This is strange, even for central London, where everyone is trying to make a living.

Outside, the air is bitingly cold. Pedestrians weave like skittles between the lines of traffic, their hands sunk deep into coat pockets, their faces wrapped in woollen scarves. The lights of the cars and buses stretch down towards Hyde Park Corner. In the chemist's shop on the Circus, a tired girl hunches over the counter and stares blankly at the busy street. In front of her, an elderly woman is pursing her lips in the cosmetics mirror. Her fur coat shines like silver under the shop's fluorescent lights.

Michael is early, of course. He hates unpunctuality, and he knows people are impressed by his time-keeping. He reckons you don't have to abandon all your principles when you're on the Social.

The studio where the society meets every other Friday evening is in a narrow alley off the north side of the Circus. It's just a black line on the *A-Z*, but Michael finds it, between an all-night bureau de change and a cigarette kiosk. It's all cracked paving slabs and tattered bin bags, oozing vegetable peelings. John would have nodded and said, 'I told you so,' and even Michael wonders if he shouldn't leave his personal details at the bureau de change, just in case.

The alley ends suddenly at a brick wall. To the right is an open door: beyond, an unshaded light bulb illuminates a dirty hallway. Brown paint is peeling from the woodwork, and the faded, floral wallpaper hangs in wispy tatters from the walls. A huge black cobweb swings gently from the light fitting and a row of milk bottles stands by the staircase, stained yellow with congealed milk. The place smells of piss.

Someone has pinned a notice on the wall which reads *Baron von Gloeden Society*, the words underlined with a wobbly arrow. The sign must originally have pointed up the stairs, but one of the pins has gone and it points down towards the milk bottles and the rotting floorboards.

He remembers the man in the suit who'd given him his card at Victoria. He'd told him to go up to the first floor where everyone would be waiting for him in the studio. Michael climbs the bare stairs. There's a door to the left and a second straight ahead. On the right, another staircase leads up to a further floor. For a moment he remains still. He can hear the faint sound of a drum beating somewhere above him, and a child crying. There's a streak of light coming from under the door ahead, and a low hum of voices. This is it.

Michael opens the door and all conversation ceases immediately. Six enquiring faces turn to greet him.

George is the group secretary, so he performs the introductions. The other members flock round Michael, their faces shining like children round a Christmas tree. Michael smiles a lot and says amusing things. He tells them he's done it all before. There won't be any problems. He stands in the centre of the room and allows himself to be watched. He looks at the rolls of coloured backing paper and the strange bits of photographic equipment, and wonders what's going to happen.

George is the friendly type. He doesn't just look at your face when he speaks to you: he looks you all over.

'You mustn't worry about us!' he says. 'We're all quite harmless! A bit mad, perhaps, but harmless!' George has a knack of putting at least one exclamation mark at the end of every sentence.

He looks about fifty – younger than most of the others. The hem of his left trouser leg has come unstitched and catches under his heel when he walks. There's a strand of cotton on the lapel of his black corduroy jacket, which no one else seems to have noticed. Someone is smelling strongly of sweet aftershave.

'What we usually do is work for about an hour, then have a quick break,' George says. 'Don't worry – we won't have you doing anything too strenuous! No swinging from the ceiling or anything!'

Michael glances up at the crumbling plaster. He's brought three pairs of shorts with him, and a singlet borrowed from John. Under his jeans, he's wearing a jockstrap. He couldn't think of anything else to bring.

'It's amazing,' George continues, 'how Ian keeps coming up with new models! He meets all of them on the street and in trains and things! I sometimes wonder how he's escaped being attacked – I mean, they're not all charming young men like you!' He winks at Michael and fiddles with a large gold umbrella. Michael wonders if it's a prop but George explains that it's something to do with reflecting light.

'Yes,' he says, 'Ian's quite a talent scout!'

'Like Hughie Green,' Michael suggests. This has everyone roaring with laughter.

'How very apt!' a voice from the corner of the room calls. It's Percy, plump and elderly, whose stomach expands like a vacuum-cleaner bag when he laughs. Michael looks at him and waits for the button on his red waistcoat to burst. Then Denis, thin, slightly younger and with a toupee, suggests that George could be Monica Rose.

Michael doesn't understand, but the others' memories stretch further, and they shriek with laughter.

Michael watches them set up their photographic equipment. It all seems very complicated. There are leads to plug in, flash bulbs to check and light angles to arrange – all of it done in a babble of gossip and giggling. George tries to supervise, but nobody really seems to know what he's doing. There are good-humoured disagreements about whose turn it is to start the session, who has the storeroom key, and who is going to change the backing paper. It's all a novelty to Michael, but he wants to get on.

There's a paraffin stove by the door which fills the air with fumes and makes him cough. No one else seems to have noticed, but the room is beginning to feel very stuffy. He realises he's sweating. It hadn't occurred to him to bring a towel, and now he begins to worry about dripping from the armpits all over the backing paper. It wouldn't look too smart showing his under-arm hair congealing in greasy rat-tails – that would be curtains for his career. He begins to think modelling might not be so easy after all. George comes to his rescue:

'Now Michael,' he says, 'we're nearly ready. There's a room off the corridor for you to change in. You'll find a towel in there – if you need one!' He's almost pinning Michael against the wall. He looks hungry. 'Did Ian ask you to bring any gear?' Michael opens his rucksack and shows him the shorts and singlet. George is delighted.

'Oh lovely!' he says, running his fingers over the shorts. 'Very nice! I'm sure you'll look a wow in these!' He winks. The fumes from the paraffin heater are beginning to give Michael a headache.

'I think we'll start you off in the singlet and these cycling shorts – oh yes, and these white socks and trainers. They're rather chunky, aren't they! Look everyone, doesn't Michael have large feet!'

Everyone crowds around Michael once again. They

decide unanimously that he does, indeed, have large feet. They're so masculine and . . . large.

The air is cold and damp out on the landing. Michael waits for a moment and breathes deeply to clear his head. Then he opens the second door and finds a light switch. The changing room is little more than a toilet, though someone theatrical has, at some time, surrounded the cracked mirror with coloured light bulbs. They no longer work. Beside the basin is a wicker chair with a grubby towel draped over the back. The cold tap works but when Michael tries to turn the hot tap, the sink begins to judder and a pipe near the ceiling rattles loose plaster from the wall.

Michael pulls his trousers off quickly. He half expects George to slip into the room and offer assistance, so he jams his arse against the door and pulls the cycling shorts from the rucksack. It feels strange wearing shorts in the middle of winter. Even at the gym, he wears a tracksuit from October to April. Still, standing almost naked in a freezing lavatory has done wonders for his perspiration problem: goose pimples are already forming across his chest.

Michael pauses again on the landing. He listens to the voices beyond the door, and to the other, fainter noises from the upper floors. The cold air wraps itself, like cool arms, round his body. A door opens upstairs, and a narrow shaft of light darts across the staircase. He hears a man's voice saying thank you; then the door is closed and heavy footsteps begin to ascend the bare wooden stairs. The voice belongs to a country parson at a summer fete, or a professor by his study fire. It sounds out of place.

Michael makes an impressive entrance. Everyone murmurs approval, and George flies around the room checking that everything is working properly.

'It's only fair,' he says, 'for such a promising model. It's a pity Ian can't be here because he really does deserve a vote of thanks for coming up with the goods yet again. He has to work late at the office this evening but he'll see everyone in the pub after the session.'

A roll of red backing paper has been unfurled and spread across half the floor. Michael is asked to stand in the centre of the paper with a small black box. It's the light meter, George explains. It tells you if you've got the right amount of light in the room. Michael stands and faces his audience. They look a strange bunch from where he's standing. For the first time, it occurs to him that it could all be a big con. How is he to know that the cameras have any film in them? He's read about that sort of thing in the Sunday papers. Perhaps all the careful preparation has been part of a big, kinky game. Michael doesn't like to think he might be taken for a ride; but he comforts himself with the prospect of the thirty quid he'll have in his pocket later.

George says they'll try some test shots before attempting anything artistic. He sounds quite serious. He tells Michael to stand quite still, just as he is. There are a few seconds of silence, then a rapid series of clicks and flashes.

'Are we going?' asks Andrew, obviously the oldest among them, who has positioned himself on a chair in the centre of the group.

'Come along, Andrew,' George says.

There is a full minute of intense concentration as Andrew attempts to hold his camera steady, then a click.

'Did I flash?'

'You didn't flash!' George says. 'Oh Andrew, how *maddening*! Never mind; have another go on the next one.'

They commiserate with Andrew and wind on their cameras.

'It didn't flash. . .' Andrew says.

George asks Michael to turn to the right. There are excited comments about dramatic shading and highlights. Michael is told that on no account must he move, because one of the straps of his jockstrap is showing, and it really does look very artistic.

Another series of clicks and flashes. Andrew is successful this time, and his companions congratulate him warmly. Michael begins to relax. They're all as nutty as fruitcakes, he decides, but they're harmless enough. He's enjoying being admired.

Then Roger – the joker in the group, who reminds Michael of a TV comedian whose name he can't recall – tells him to move back slightly but to stay in the same position. Michael steps carefully backwards.

'Stop!' George cries. 'Oh poetry! Just look at that.'
'Oh, I say!' another says. 'The shading! The contrasts!'
'I thought so,' Roger says.
There is another burst of camera fire.
'I've got something on my lens,' Andrew says.
'No, Andrew, you *can't* have!'
'What's that on his leg?'
'Where?'
'There – under his shorts. Is it a scar, or have I got something on my lens?'
'It's the end of his jockstrap, Andrew,' George explains.
'Oh,' Andrew replies. 'Well, can't he tuck it in? I'm surprised no one noticed.'
George sighs. 'Perhaps you'd better tuck it in, Michael.'

The session progresses. He removes his singlet and then his shorts. The atmosphere crackles. He poses looking left and looking right, standing up and sitting down, kneeling, squatting and leaning across a chair. Everything goes perfectly until Roger asks him to put his hands on his head and stand on one leg, naked.

'Eh?'
'It's one of my favourites,' Roger explains.

When Michael removes his jockstrap, the room is so quiet, you can hear the baby crying upstairs. He attempts to balance his weight on his right leg and tuck his left leg up towards his back. He trembles violently and falls down. A murmur of sympathy ripples through the group, and he tries again. This time, a searing cramp rips through the back of his right thigh.

'The model we had last time managed it all right,' Andrew says helpfully.

'He was a professional dancer, Andrew,' George reminds him.

'Was he really?'

'We told you he was – remember? You asked him where he'd got his calves. . .'

'Oh yes.' Andrew seems amused. He starts chuckling and then chokes so violently he has to retire to the corner of the room for a few minutes.

They beg Michael to try standing on one leg again. He's reluctant, but he thinks of the money. The prospect of those crisp tenners gives his right leg unexpected strength. He succeeds. They stand and watch him.

'Lovely!' George says, clapping his hands.

'Very good,' Roger says, nodding slowly. 'That's the one.'

'Well, get on with it!' Michael exclaims. He can feel his right leg going into spasm.

His audience clicks and flashes.

'Can I go now?' Andrew asks, shuffling back to the centre of the group.

'Jesus!'

'Yes, do, Andrew,' George says.

There's another pause as Andrew takes focus; then a click.

'Did I flash?'

'I don't know.'

'I don't think I flashed.'

'You didn't flash,' Michael says, bringing his left leg down to the floor with a thud.

Andrew doesn't seem especially anxious to try again, and George hurries the group on to a less demanding pose. By the door, the flames of the paraffin heater flicker blue and yellow as people hurry past on the landing. Every so often, the fumes waft across the room, but Michael is too busy thinking of the money to notice. He knows he should buy ten pounds' worth of Telecom stamps, but he knows he'll buy the black Adidas tracksuit he saw on the way to the studio instead.

The session finishes in a haze of flashing lights and paraffin fumes, and Michael hurries back into the grubby changing room. He's in a hurry: his balls are in danger of freezing off and there's still the possibility of George rushing in and trying something funny. He puts the jockstrap and shorts back on, and then his jeans. It's even colder than when he arrived.

When he returns to the studio, he finds everyone packing up. Again it strikes him as a real performance for just a couple of hours of photography. He wonders what they do with the photos. Surely Andrew doesn't wank over smutty photos at his time of life? He seems to have enough trouble fitting his camera into its case. . .

Ian's arrived. He's wearing the suit he had on when Michael first saw him at Victoria, and he's still carrying the grey umbrella. He's warming his hands in front of the fire and chatting to George.

'He *did* do well,' George says, as Michael joins them by the fire. 'I hope we'll be seeing more of Michael.'

Ian seems relieved that the evening has been a success. You can never be quite sure with an unknown quantity.

'Well, his quantity's certainly no mystery now!' George winks. Ian manages to grimace sympathetically without George noticing, and he asks if Michael will join them for a drink. All Michael wants to do is catch the bus home, but he knows it'll look a bit bad if he hurries off immediately. He wishes he'd thought of an excuse at the beginning of the evening, but it's too late now. He accepts.

He wonders what John is doing back at the flat. For someone so stupid, he has a very vivid imagination. He thinks Michael's a mug talking to strange men in the street, and even dafter going off to an address near Piccadilly to "model". Michael amuses himself with the thought that John has probably contacted Interpol or phoned the Salvation Army's missing persons service. He won't have phoned the police, of course: he has a career in accountancy to think about.

They go to a pub off Leicester Square. It's just been Victorianised, with lots of gleaming brass-work, fake gas lamps and synthetic, easy-sweep sawdust on the floor. A glass-fronted counter displays anaemic sandwiches, attractively interspersed with slightly unripe tomatoes and lumps of cheese. The beer is disgusting.

One corner of the pub has been taken over by a group of young soldiers. Their rucksacks and cases suggest they're going off on leave. You can tell, even without the evidence of their baggage, that they're squaddies. Every other word is an expletive, but their freshly laundered sweatshirts and immaculate jeans are perfect. They could have stepped from the pages of a mail order catalogue.

George notices the squaddies and looks at little else for the next hour. Michael feels uncomfortable: flirting with a model who's dropping his jockstrap five yards in front of you is one thing, but drooling over a group of beer-soaked, back-slapping Army boys is another. He begins to wish he'd gone home after all. It must look strange to an outsider, him sitting with a group of men all old enough to be his father.

Of course, no one cares. Who notices anything in a pub in central London? The squaddies are busy with a belching contest; the boys and girls by the juke box are set for the Hippodrome; and the solitary drinkers along the bar are interested in no one but themselves. Even the barmaid, shimmering in a silver-sequinned blouse, might be invisible as she passes between the tables collecting empty glasses. All the trouble she's taken with her appearance, and nobody sees her.

The landlord rings the bell for last orders, and one of the soldiers rises unsteadily to his feet. He sets off for the bar, but stops abruptly by the food counter, where he claps his hand over his mouth and staggers off to the toilet. His companions jeer and call him a tosser.

Through the crowd, Michael sees the face of the barmaid as she moves backwards and forwards behind the bar. She has no real expression at all: before she's even handed back the change, she's on to the next customer. They keep on, and they won't give her a minute's rest, and even when it's all over, there's no escape from the fact that opening time is only twelve hours away. Michael looks at her and reckons there are worse ways of making money than flashing your dick around in a photographic studio every so often.

They're all taking the tube to Embankment. George is sorry that Michael's catching a bus home: he'd have loved a quiet chat on the train. Michael shrugs his shoulders and smiles.

'Next time, eh?' he says. He feels happier now he can go off on his own.

'We're having a small drinks do the week before Christmas!' George says. 'You *must* come! Ian, make sure Michael knows about our drinks do, won't you?'

They all wish him goodnight. Michael watches them disappear down the steps of the Underground station, chattering to the last, jostled by the theatre crowd and the packs of hungry young night-clubbers swarming to the Hippodrome. He feels the three crisp bank notes in his pocket again, and smiles. It's going to be easy if they're all like this. He might put an advert in the camera magazines. He might even try a bit of massage – nothing over the top, of course. They're called punters in the business, apparently. He could do it with his eyes closed.

Another Byte

I could be the only person in the world to have seen dog shit on a Swiss pavement. I saw it early yesterday morning. Not much to get excited about, as dog shit goes. It was nestling by a litter bin in the market square cobbles; a compact, slightly shiny brown curl. The air was clear and cold and I was on my way to buy croissants from the patisserie near the station.

I have a photo of it on the last roll of film. It must be sandwiched somewhere between the Catholic church frieze and the Swiss horn-player at last night's fondue-fest. I took the photo because no one back in London would ever believe me if I just told them about it. The litter bin had the name Lausanne printed on it, and something else in French, which I couldn't understand. This means there can't be any accusations of trick photography.

It was a slight enough discovery to make on a bright July morning, but it was significant. Who can resist exploding life's little myths – those strange, irrelevant ideas we accept as gospel truth all our lives? Apparently, Mussolini didn't get the trains running on time; hair doesn't grow thicker if you keep shaving it off, and now, it seems, Swiss dogs do sometimes crap on pavements. These revelations are useful when you find yourself among strangers at dinner parties and funeral teas.

Funny how we chip away at our folklore and expose it as fallacy, when what we really need is the comfort of stability. I suppose it would be pointless saying this to you, Paul Latchford. There won't be any space in your timetable for aimless reflection. There shouldn't really be any room for me on your computerised schedule; though here we are, in a foreign country, talking about

24

the old days. Perhaps even your rare holidays are committed, in neat, byte-sized portions, to floppy disc. You've surprised me by remembering so much – even things I'd forgotten. . .

We laugh when we talk about them now, and we laugh when we're alone. Yes, even you, Paul, sitting there in your crisp, baggy chinos and your expensive cotton shirt with its slim maroon stripes. You don't have much time for idle reflection these days – scarcely a moment to sit still – but you can't resist it, every now and then.

We haven't seen each other for two years, but I know all about you. Your face, crowned by a dozen subtly different hairstyles, has beamed, brooded and scowled at me from magazine covers and advertising hoardings. After you phoned me last week, when you asked to meet me here, I read about you in 'Celebrity' magazine. You'd beaten Joan Collins to the centre-spread profile. Then later, down in the Underground station, your sooty, tattered face smiled at me across the rails. You were advertising 'Slapstick Skincare' products for men. There was even a quote by you: 'Its a complete lifestyle concept'. You were never very good at possessives: that's one thing we had in common.

Yes, that's what you are now, Paolo – a complete concept; trimmed, tidied, packaged to perfection, flickering slickly on late-night satellite TV in millions of dark rooms across Europe. You're a boundary-breaker, an international touchstone, a common icon like Coca-Cola and McDonalds.

'Celebrity' ran a photo beside your centre-page profile. They caught you in careful relaxation, lying in a big bedroom, with a computer where the bedside table should be. The duvet cover was black with a silver border. You've even learned to keep your mouth slightly open for photographers.

Remember Kilburn? Remember the Noddy and Big Ears alarm clock you set for ten every signing-on day? It's far behind you now. There are no more lazy days for you, lying in bed watching 'Bewitched' repeats on the black-and-white Russian portable, no more snuggling under musty counterpanes of foxed silk with plates of boiled pasta and tuna fish. The computer's your alarm clock now. It wakes you with a click and a hum every morning, and churns out your diary on a ream of serrated paper – a laser-printed, step-by-step guide that tells you where to go, what to do, how to get there, and when to do it. It tells you how to live and how much you can afford to live.

Of course you laugh to yourself in your rare private moments: in the shower? Under the sunbed? On the toilet? Remember the days when 'concept' was part of a word on a condom packet? When your greatest challenge was trying to make sixty pounds social last a fortnight? When we sat too long at my window with mugs of scummy tea, watching the trade come and go at the chip shop over the road?

It might just be the effect of this wine on a warm afternoon; but if you really want to know, Polo, I feel a bit sick.

They were sitting outside the Café des Ecureuils, in one of the little back streets of Lausanne, near where the wooden canopied staircases leads up to the cathedral. It was a hot, still afternoon. The waiter's white shirt was wet under the arms, but his face provided such distraction that few, if anyone, had noticed. He and Steven smiled at one another each time he passed the table. Paul was leaning back in his chair, just far enough to catch the sunlight falling in a diagonal slab between the roofs of the old town. He was wearing dark glasses, but a group of students by the café door had recognised him as soon as he'd sat down. He'd carefully avoided looking in their direction for the last thirty minutes.

'So you haven't seen him, then?' he asked.

'No,' Steven said. 'I rang his number before I left London, but there was no answer. Just that funny tone foreign phones have. I couldn't tell if it was ringing, engaged or disconnected. I don't even know if he still lives in the same place.'

'It was near here, wasn't it? Didn't he live somewhere near these steps?'

Steven nodded and glanced briefly towards the

cathedral steps, where a fat woman tourist was being photographed by her fat companion.

'I remember you telling me,' Paul went on. 'You used to sit at the window at night-time, with the lights off, and listen to the sound of footsteps on the stairs.'

'That's right,' Steven said. 'And every hour through the night, the watchman walked round the tower and shouted the hour. I expect he still does. You can't hear where I'm staying this time.'

'That must have been a pain, having someone shout at you every hour of the night.'

'I didn't hear it after the third night,' Steven said, looking around him. 'I got used to all this very quickly.' He thought about it for a moment, tapping his finger on the rim of his glass.

'But I suppose it always felt like a dream.' He laughed. 'Now that was a summer when the sun really *did* shine all the time! I took my finals, and the Argie-bargies surrendered, and I came here. The sun was shining when I arrived, and it was shining when I went home in October.'

'How long were you here?'

'About four months.'

'Long dream. . .'

'It was only like a dream because I could always see the end,' Steven said. 'I remember telling one of my tutors that I was coming to Switzerland – he knew all about Claude – and he said "Enjoy yourself, because you'll never be as free again."'

'Gosh, how profound.' Paul reached for the bottle.

'But I don't think you're free when you're dreaming, are you?' Steven said.

'How melancholy. More wine.'

'Go on, then.' Steven watched Paul fill his glass. 'Is your tan real?'

'No,' Paul said. 'It's an hour on the sunbed every week. Sunbathing lost its attraction when I interviewed Miriam Stoppard for Thames last year. She went on and on about skin cancer – very nicely, of course. I'd just come back from Algeria, and she kept looking at my arms. . . So now

27

I stick to an hour a week on the sunbed, and anything else I get by way of incidental sunshine. Anyway, I don't have time for lying in the sun these days.'

'I'm glad the weather's like this,' Steven said. 'Since that summer, I've always thought of Switzerland as a hot country.'

'I saw snow in Zurich once,' Paul said. 'From the plane window. I can't remember where I'd been, but we stopped to refuel at Zurich. The snow was going sideways past the window. It looked freezing.'

'It would have spoilt it, if I'd come here and found it raining.'

'Why did you come here?'

Steven looked at him. 'I told you,' he said. 'I'm on my way to Italy for a holiday – meeting friends in Rome. They don't get there till Sunday. I decided to take an extra two days off work and travel a bit first. I can go anywhere I like with my railcard. . .'

'But you chose to come here. . .'

'It's on the way.'

'Well, sort of.'

Steven laughed. 'Yeah, a bit of nostalgia, I suppose. Anyway, it's meant we've seen each other again.'

'You must have been surprised to hear my voice on the phone,' Paul said.

'I was, a bit,' Steven said. 'I thought at first you might be offering me a job.'

They laughed at the idea.

'Sounds like you're doing all right where you are – video distributors, isn't it?'

'Yeah,' Steven said. 'PR and advertising. Being nice to people.'

'I bet you're good at that,' Paul said. He meant it. 'You find it easy to be nice.'

'I don't, really,' Steven said. 'What gets me is how *grateful* people are when you're nice to them. There's something a bit pathetic about it. Do you know what I mean?'

'No,' Paul said, 'not really.'

'Anyway,' Steven continued, 'you're the real professional as far as dealing with people is concerned. Look at you!' He looked Paul up and down. 'You're the epitome of satellite communication – it said so in *Celebrity* magazine.'

'Oh God, did you read it?'

'An Olympic runner for the twenty-first century, spreading your message across Europe.'

They laughed again.

'But I don't have a message,' Paul said. 'My only function is to get other people to talk about themselves. That's the whole point about doing chat shows and interviews. It's not *me* they want. I'm just a microphone.'

'But you're a star! Look at the reaction you've caused with them over there.' Steven glanced across to the table by the café door, where the group of students continued to watch them closely.

'I've been trying not to since we arrived,' Paul said, shifting further round in his chair.

'Perhaps they're wondering if I'm your boyfriend,' Steven said.

'Anyway,' Paul said, 'you're wrong. You *are* nice to people, whether you're at work or not. I'm just a professional.'

'Well, you're certainly that. . .'

The fat tourists finished their roll of film with a deftly-angled shot of the man against a backdrop of hanging flower baskets. They flopped down at the next table. The waiter with the wet armpits smoothed his white apron at the café door and wove between the tables to where they were sitting. When the man ordered cassis in drawling French, the waiter licked his pencil deftly and scribbled on the pad that hung around his waist. On his way back to the bar, he glanced again at Steven, and this time he frowned slightly.

'Well, you're the star here,' Paul said, with a crooked smile. It was one of the expressions that had made him a television celebrity across Europe. Steven couldn't recall him ever having smiled that way in the old days. 'Do you still want dinner with me, or should I slip away and let you wait for his shift to end?'

'I never waited for any man's shift to end,' Steven

said. The fat woman looked up from her magazine. 'I suppose he might know something about Claude, if I asked him. We drank here a few times.' Steven looked towards the wooden steps. 'His apartment was just there. Third floor.'

'You are funny,' Paul said. 'I can't believe you've come all this way and got so close, and then you sit here wondering if you should contact the guy. He could be at home now.'

The idea hadn't occurred to Steven. He shifted uncomfortably in his seat.

'No,' he said. 'He'll probably be in Geneva. I know he's studying architecture there now.'

'But he hasn't moved?'

'I don't think so. I don't know. The few postcards he sends never have an address. It makes me wonder if he'd want to see me again.'

'I suppose you can't really go back. . .' Paul said, resting his chin on his hands and looking pensive.

'Christ, you sound like Celia Johnson,' Steven said. 'Anyway, he's had a boyfriend for the past year or so – he said so on his last card.'

'Why should that stop you?'

'I don't know.'

The waiter returned. He placed the bottle and glasses in front of the man and woman and glanced again at Steven. He looked vaguely puzzled.

'It was fun last night, wasn't it?' Paul said. 'I thought fondue went out with AIDS.'

'It was all for the tourists,' Steven said. 'I mean, remember that band? Swiss people don't really go around tarted up like that.'

'Only if it makes them money. Did you notice the cuckoo clock in the hotel reception?'

'*And* it's one of the most exclusive hotels in town. It's mentioned in my *Blue Guide*,' Steven said.

'Of course,' Paul replied. 'Where else would a famous television personality stay?'

'Did the computer book it for you?'

Paul laughed. 'The name came up on the computer, yes.'

Steven shook his head. 'What a life!'

'It was pretty creepy at first, but it was written into my contract. I suppose it makes sense. Last year I made a hundred trips to Europe. My company thought it was a good investment. No missed flights or clashing appointments.' He paused for a moment and peered into his glass. 'And, of course, when they first saw me, I'd come straight from Kilburn on the bus. I suppose they realised I was hopeless at organising things myself.'

'But don't you resent all that interference in your life?'

Paul smiled and shrugged his shoulders. 'But it *is* my life. Where would I be now if this hadn't happened? Still lying in bed in Kilburn, farting under the mattress all day. I was never like you, Steve. I know neither of us had a job or any money, but you always had an imagination. You had somewhere else to go. Remember when I used to call round at yours? You were always doing something – writing those trashy porn stories or painting the kitchen walls. And even when you were staring out of the window, your brain was going like the clappers about something. You left me behind. I had nothing like that to keep me going.'

'How *did* you get that job?'

'I went to bed with two of the directors of the production company,' Paul said, matter-of-factly. 'We had a three-way. I didn't know if I was meant to enjoy myself or not, so I acted dumb, and it worked. In the end, I suppose, my face just fitted.'

'Are we still talking about the three-way?'

They paid the girl at the cash desk just inside the café door. Steven looked around for the waiter, but he couldn't see him. It was nearly five o'clock and the café was filling with people just out of work. Three copies of a local evening paper, strung on batons and stamped with the café logo of a squirrel with a hazelnut, were being passed around the tables. When they stepped back outside, the sun was slipping behind the red tiled roofs of the old town. The narrow street echoed with the sound of laughter and the rumble of metal shutters being lowered across shop windows.

Before they turned the corner, Steven took a look back at the café, but the waiter had disappeared. The fat man and the fat woman were engrossed in magazines, the woman's pink, puffy arms stretched across the table top like slabs of salmon mousse. Only the small group of students, craning and stretching their necks to see beyond the other customers, noticed them leave.

Steven walked Paul as far as the row of benches by the giant cheeseboard of grey and white paving stones. Two young men were playing chess. They had long, straggly hair and beards, and both wore ripped jeans and grubby white t-shirts. One of them stood with his arms drawn up round his chest. He was smoking a curved briar pipe and gazing across to the far end of the square. His companion squatted by the chessboard, deep in concentration. On the bench beside them were two patchwork shoulder bags made of purple velvet and other fragments of frayed material. Next to the bags was a scratched tin of Dutch tobacco, a packet of cigarette papers and a white personal stereo. Paul laughed quietly and turned to Steven.

'In London it'd be a black leather holdall and a plastic bag full of crack. That's what I like about the Swiss. The world is just too fast and confusing for them. They're always a few crucial steps behind.'

Steven laughed. 'More confusing than for the rest of us?'

'Well, maybe they don't know how to hide things like we do. I don't know.'

Steven didn't say anything. He was smiling down towards a bare patch of cobbles beside a nearby litter bin. Something seemed to have amused him.

He watched Paul walk away across the square, and then he glanced at his watch. After a moment or two of thought, he walked back in the direction of the cathedral and the Café des Ecureuils.

Steven slept for an hour back at the hotel. He dreamt he was working in a chip shop near a building site. When the site workers trudged in, he beckoned them, one by one, to come behind the counter, and then he took them into a back room. He tried to look at the men's faces, but their features liquified and swam out of focus, and when he attempted to remove their soiled jeans, the zips jammed. Four men followed him into the back room, and four times the zips jammed. None of the men walked out: they just melted into the wall. Steven could feel Paul's presence somewhere in the room, silent and invisible, as if wrapped around him in the darkness, and a silent vibration of his faraway laughter. The back of his neck was stinging when he woke. He'd spent too long in the sun and his head ached.

The bathroom had white tiles on the walls and white tiles on the floor. The floor sloped gently from all four sides to a central drainage hole. There was a shower nozzle and taps near the ceiling on one wall, and a white porcelain sink with a mirror above it. Two fluffy white towels hung from a rail on the back of the door. Steven closed the door and turned on the shower and then the hot tap in the sink. The room became a Turkish bath, the tiles and the mirror disappearing behind clouds of white steam. He stood with his feet astride the plug-hole, feeling the steam melt in warm trickles across his shoulders, and he tried to work out which bits of Paul he recognised. He wanted to find two men; but for now, he stood wrapped in thick steam, invisible and out of reach, in the centre of Europe.

They had dinner in the hotel dining room, at a table near the French windows. The trees in the hotel garden were threaded with strings of light bulbs that turned the grass white. Car horns hooted in the street beyond the garden, and an orchestra was playing somewhere in the distance. Paul had dressed for dinner. Steven hadn't come on holiday expecting dinners in expensive hotels; he wore his clean pair of jeans and a crumpled white shirt he'd found at the bottom of his holdall. Everyone else in the restaurant looked very smart.

Between courses, a young woman in a black dress walked over to their table. She smiled at them and passed Paul a cordless telephone.

'I'm sorry, Paul,' she said. 'Gordon's on the line from London. There's some change to the timetable tomorrow. The Italians won't be arriving until after lunch.'

'Sod it!' Paul stood up. 'Listen, I'll take this in reception, all right?'

The girl looked worried. 'I'm sorry,' she said. 'I didn't want to spoil your dinner. . .' She glanced at Steven, who smiled.

'No, it's all right, Judy. I just wish I could get away from the phone – just for one evening.' He turned to Steven. 'I'm sorry, I won't be long.'

'Take your time,' Steven said. 'You want cheesecake?'

'Lemon sorbet.'

'But you always had cheesecake.'

A thin smile passed across Paul's face. 'Computer says it's too fattening. See you in a minute.'

He was away for almost fifteen minutes. When he returned, the sorbet had melted to a pool of sticky fruit juice in the bottom of the bowl.

'I'm sorry,' Steven said. 'I thought you'd be back sooner.'

'It's all right. I'll make do with coffee.' He seemed agitated.

'Problems?'

'Oh, just organisational ones,' Paul said. 'You know we're covering this fashion festival next week. The Italians are going to be the real stars, and they've just told the organisers they'll be arriving late tomorrow and no one will be available for interview until the day after. It's just a pain in the arse.' He beckoned to a passing waiter and ordered coffee.

'So, why have you come here so early?' Steven asked.

Paul smiled and shrugged his shoulders. 'The computer

said I could have a few days' holiday. I was going to come here early anyway, and then when I discovered you'd be here as well, I thought . . . well, it seemed like a good idea.'

'Who was the girl?'

'Judy? She's one of the PR people. There are five of us here altogether.'

'She seemed nervous.'

'She wants to be my secretary.'

'I see.'

'But the way she looks at me makes me nervous. I don't know why she does it: they all know about me. She must realise it's a waste of time.'

Steven leaned back in his chair and spooned the froth off his coffee. 'So how long do you think all this'll last?'

'I don't know,' Paul said. 'Not very long. It's that kind of job. I've made lots of contacts over the last couple of years, so I'll be able to do something. I suppose it's never seemed like a real job because I've always known it won't last that long. What about you?'

'Oh, *mine* won't last long,' Steven said. 'They took me on for three months, while someone was off sick. Then they kept me on for another month, and then another. I haven't got a contract, and I'm still on emergency tax, but it beats staring out of the window all day. Every day I expect them to tell me I'm leaving at the end of the week. I think it'll happen soon. That's why I took a holiday while I had the money.'

'And then?'

'I don't know, really, but I've got a few ideas. . .'

'I wish you could meet someone you liked,' Paul said. 'I always thought that.'

'I was seeing a radio producer for a while last year,' Steven said. 'He lived in a converted warehouse in Bermondsey. He was into flavoured condoms – that was quite interesting. The stairs got me down in the end – there was no lift. We were getting on all right, I suppose. At least he was so busy we only saw each other once or twice a week, which seemed very civilised. Then, one evening I went round to dinner

35

and he got drunk and told me he never wanted me to go away.'

'What happened?'

'I caught the bus home and wrote him a letter. That was in February. I haven't heard from him since, but I suppose I will eventually. I'd like to see him again socially.'

Paul laughed. 'You're just the same!' he said. 'I knew you wouldn't have changed.'

'I don't suppose I have.'

'You probably think I've changed completely.'

'Well, not completely. . .' Steven smiled. 'Anyway, where's your glamorous boyfriend? I thought you'd have someone with you here.'

'There was someone, back in London,' Paul said. 'He lived with me for a while, but it didn't work out. I was never at home. He was twenty-two, but he wanted to settle down.'

Steven laughed. 'I sometimes envy people who want to settle down.'

'He actually enjoyed playing the martyred housewife bit. The final straw was when I got home from a trip and found he'd unplugged the computer to hoover the bedroom carpet. It fucked up a whole disc full of diary appointments. He admitted he'd done it out of spite. At least he was realistic enough to see it wasn't working out. He was a nice boy – we parted on good terms. The company was furious: they said I should have made him sign a promise not to sell anything to the Sunday papers.' He laughed ironically. 'That summed up their attitude, as far as I was concerned. I told them I knew he wouldn't do anything like that, but they saw it differently. Besides, it wouldn't have done me any harm if he *had* spoken to the papers. You could tell them much more interesting things about my past.'

'That's true. Perhaps I'll go back to my hotel now and start writing.'

'I was hoping we might sleep together,' Paul said. 'Just like we used to when one of us missed the last bus home. The bed here is much more comfortable than anything either of us had then.'

'Won't the hotel mind?'

'They'll be thrilled,' Paul said. 'I think they were expecting sex 'n' drugs, wild media parties and lots of after-hours door slamming. We must have been quite a let-down. What time's your train tomorrow?'

'Not until two. I won't be in a hurry.'

'Neither will I, now the Italians are arriving late.'

'Does your computer allow this kind of casual deviation?'

Paul laughed. 'You think it's crazy, don't you?'

'I think it's a bit creepy.'

'Steven, away from the computer I'm as hopeless as ever.'

Judy returned as they were leaving their table.

'I'm sorry, Paul. Glenn's on the line from London. He's got hold of some Italian shoe designer who he thinks you ought to talk to tomorrow.'

Paul sighed. 'I'll be right with you.'

'I'm sorry. . .'

'It's all right – really.'

Judy hurried out of the dining room.

'I'd better go and see what it's all about,' Paul said. 'I'll try not to be too long.'

Steven glanced at his watch. 'Look,' he said, 'I'll stroll down to the lake. I could do with a bit of fresh air. Shall I meet you back in reception in half an hour?'

'Well, I could do with some air too. Why don't you. . ?'

But Judy was standing by the reception desk with the phone in her hand, watching him.

'Yeah, OK. If I know Glenn, he'll take for ever. See you in a bit.'

The boy was waiting for him at the bandstand where the trees formed a canopy across the lakeside path. Steven had once sat there with Claude, watching the boys skateboard by. He remembered them now and wondered what they were all doing. Some of them would be fathers now, he supposed: some would be clean-cut business men in smart suits, plotting to steal British chocolate in air-conditioned board rooms. It was very dark away from the promenade lights, and Steven could just make out the boy's silhouette on the wooden steps. The air smelled of grass and stagnant water. Small waves slapped against the concrete breakwater beyond the trees. It was very warm. The boy was wearing shorts and a black vest.

'I can't stay long,' Steven said. 'I have to get back to my friend.'

'You told me he wasn't your friend,' the boy said, good-naturedly.

'We've known each other a long time. He's a bit unhappy this evening. I think he wants to talk to me.'

'Ah.' The boy pulled Steven into a gap between the bandstand and a thick clump of bushes and kissed him on the lips. 'I wanted to do that six years ago,' he said. 'I hated Claude for being able to do it.'

'I'm sorry,' Steven said. 'I've tried to think back, but I'm afraid I don't remember you.'

The boy laughed quietly. 'It doesn't matter. We only spoke to each other twice – when you and Claude came to the bar where I was working then. Why should you have noticed anyone else when you were with Claude?'

'Do you see him?' Steven asked. 'Is he still here?'

'He still has the flat,' the boy replied, 'but he's not there very much. His friend lives in Geneva, and he's working there most of the time. He's doing very well, I think.'

They kissed again, but Steven wanted to know more.

'Does he still look the same?'

The boy laughed. 'Yes, of course. He is still as handsome as before. I always liked him, but he was never interested in me. I use to have fantasies about you and him together – a few of us at the bar did. You know, at the café this afternoon, I couldn't decide who you were for quite a while. I just knew I recognised you, and I couldn't remember where from.'

'Have you seen his boyfriend?'

'He was pointed out to me once. He is tall and handsome, like the others.'

'Others?'

'After you went away, there were others. This one has

38

lasted quite a long time. I suppose they're still together. Like I say, I never see them. By the way, my name is Thierry.'

'Hi, Terry.'

'Why don't you take off your clothes?'

'I don't have long. I think my friend needs me. . .'

'I don't take long.'

'Fair enough.'

The wheels of a skateboard rattled past on the path, invisible in the darkness.

So maybe I'll still be around somewhere, Polo, the day you switch off that computer; and we can get back into bed with our plates of pasta and the evening paper folded open at the telly page. You won't have to hurry out of bed on cold winter afternoons to change the channels, but otherwise things will be very much as they were.

The train will cross the border into Italy in twenty minutes, and I don't suppose I'll go to Switzerland again. I have the camera wrapped in boxer shorts in the middle of my rucksack, and a roll of film to remind me of the last three days. I was wrong: you haven't really changed at all. In the railway station at Lausanne, I bought the new issue of 'Celebrity'. I missed a few minutes of scenery reading about Joan Collins, but it didn't fool me. You can't believe half what you're told.

Buried Treasure

She's sitting at the usual bench under the arches – a little early this week: the clock up in the library tower hasn't yet struck twelve thirty. She's wearing the same pleated skirt, the same brown tweed coat, unbuttoned despite the wind. Her tights are red today. The grubby Tupperware box is open on her lap, and she's feeding the pigeons. She hasn't seen him; but if he watches her much longer, he knows he'll see her look round and watch the people coming out of the library door. One day, one of these unvarying, identical Saturdays, he'll give her the slip and she won't see him any more.

A hand touches him on the shoulder. It's Mr Thaw, the chief librarian.

'Didn't see you in there this morning, Mr Comber.'

Close up, he looks even more like an overgrown child.

'I've been in the records office. I haven't been into the reading room yet. I thought you might be wondering where I was.'

'Well, I'm pleased to see you,' the librarian says. Outside the hushed library, his voice is still smooth and soothing, like thick cream pouring from a jug. 'Saturday mornings aren't the same without you around. Of course, the library attracts more young people during the holidays. Far too many, for my liking. We prefer dealing with the older regulars like yourself. We missed you this morning.'

'How touching.' Patronising young bugger!

'Of course, the Duchess paid her usual visit. . .'

They look towards the bench. A dozen or so pigeons are strutting around at the woman's feet, darting over

40

the flagstones as she throws tiny scraps of bread from the Tupperware box. Her grey hair is blowing across her face, but she doesn't seem to have noticed.

'It feels like rain,' Mr Thaw says. 'Don't you think so?'

'Yes, I think it does.'

'I don't like that wind. I'll swear it means rain. I'm off to the south coast with my fiancée later today – sailing. . .'

'Oh yes?'

'Her father owns a yacht. It's a break for me, you see, being cooped up in there all the time.'

One of the security guards hurries up the steps, a radio crackling from the pocket of his jacket. Mr Thaw looks at him enquiringly, but the guard just arches his eyebrows wearily and hurries past into the museum.

'They keep on their toes, those boys,' Mr Thaw says. 'There's always *something* going on here. You wouldn't think it, would you? Libraries always seem such quiet places. How is your research going, Mr Comber?'

'Oh . . . steadily, you know. No hurry. . .'

'That's the way. I sometimes look at some of the university crowd hunched over their books – concentrating so hard they look as if they're in pain.' He grimaces. 'You're just the sort who'd benefit from a mature degree course, if you don't mind me saying so. A studious, thoughtful type of person like you. . .'

'Yes, I sometimes think. . .'

'You ought to *think* about it, anyway.'

The woman's seen them. She scrapes the hair back from her face and waves at them, grinning. The pigeons dart out across the flagstones and watch her, beady-eyed and stupid-looking, under the arches.

'Near to finding that hidden treasure,' Mr Thaw says. 'She confessed as much to me this morning – only don't let on I told you. I think it's all very *hush-hush*!' His pale cheeks go round and puffy when he laughs, like white marshmallows. It's difficult to imagine his white skin burning in a sea breeze.

'She's a strange person. . . Well, I must go. Lunch calls. Will you be in later?'

'Yes, I may. . .' he says. 'I have a few friends to visit later on. I'm not sure. . .'

'That's right – keep busy. Always on the move! I envy you working for yourself, Mr Comber, I really do. A free spirit. And look at me!'

And he hurries away, down the steps and across the museum forecourt, the tails of his raincoat flapping in the chilly breeze.

She won't offer him one of her tiny sandwiches. That's one thing she's given up trying.

'I thought your wife must be unwell, Mr Comber,' she says. 'Or that one of your children had come to stay for the Easter weekend, perhaps.'

'No, no.' He sits down at the far end of the bench. 'I was working in the records office most of the morning. I thought you might wonder. . .'

The woman looks at him intently. Her pale blue eyes still surprise him, after all this time.

'Oh I did!' she says. 'I *did* wonder. I asked Oscar if *he'd* seen you.'

They look across towards the pillars.

'Now remind me. . .' he begins.

'Oh Mr Comber!' He can hear cigarette tar in her laugh. 'How many times do I have to tell you?'

'I know,' he says, bowing his head in mock shame. 'You know how forgetful I am.'

'Oscar is the one furthest away from us – with the touch of brown on the tail feathers.'

'Ah yes. . .' He doesn't see a pigeon with any brown in its tail feathers. He'd like to see them all shot. He could do it himself, quite easily.

'They saw you first, today,' the woman says. 'They told me you were over there, talking to Mr Thaw. I hadn't noticed.' She leaned towards him slightly. 'Now I hope Mr Thaw didn't *say* anything?'

'Say?'

'About me! About my *news*!'

'Nothing,' he says innocently, reaching into his battered briefcase for a sandwich. 'What news is that?'

42

Two young security guards emerge from the library and stand against a pillar. One lights a cigarette and passes it to his friend. Then he lights one for himself. The second guard speaks into a radio and scans the museum forecourt through narrowed eyes.

'Well, would you believe it!' the woman exclaims. 'Just as I was about to tell you of my discovery.'

'I don't think they can hear from where they are.'

'Microphones!' she replies. 'Bugs!' She leans further towards him and whispers through her hair. 'The fact is, I think I'm close to tracing the fortune!'

'Well, that's wonderful news.'

'Shh!' Her finger catches in her hair. 'Don't speak too loudly!'

He looks at the guards again. They're taking a break, that's all.

'There's more than usual around this morning. Haven't you noticed?'

Now she comes to mention it, he has.

'It's the IRA,' he says. 'Security. Public places.'

'They're after my fortune!' she retorts, biting into one of her sandwiches. He notices a paper doily at the bottom of the Tupperware box. 'They're after what's rightfully mine! They're working for the other lot.'

'Your cousins?' He's heard the story a hundred times.

The woman nods. 'Somehow they've found out I'm close to discovering the truth!'

A middle-aged man walks up the steps and into the museum and smiles briefly at them. He's one of the regular visitors. He spends a lot of time reading the periodicals by the reading room exit. He leaves the reading room for short periods of time at least twice every visit. Gerald's noticed, though the man does it as quietly as he can. One afternoon, Gerald looked up from his novel to see the man staring strangely at him from over *The Financial Times*. They'd never spoken.

'Did you see those trousers?' the woman says. 'On a man his age!'

'Tell me what you've discovered,' Gerald says.

'I can't go into details here,' she replies. 'But I can say that my work will soon be finished!'

He pummels his sandwich until one corner of the white bread is thick and sticky between his fingers.

'You won't be coming her any more?'

'Well, I won't need to, will I?' the woman says. 'When I've got my last bit of evidence – of how those shysters robbed me of my home and fortune – I'll be able to go to the police.' She closes her eyes, as she does whenever she imagines the end of her quest, and leans back. For a moment, he feels almost as if he's alone on the bench. A particularly strong gust of wind scours across the flagstones and chills his ankles.

'I haven't forgotten what I promised you, Mr Comber,' she says softly, her eyes still closed.

'Oh?' Gerald says. 'What was that?'

She leans forward and looks at him.

'About inviting you and Mrs Comber to stay with me at my home in the country! You won't believe how beautiful it is. It's a different world to all this. . . I do hope you'll come. I've heard so much about Mrs Comber.'

Gerald smiles. 'She's made some of her congress tarts,' he says. 'Would you like one?'

She giggles like a girl. He's noticed it before. She doesn't need to say yes.

'You don't know how gratifying it's been having you to talk to every Saturday,' she says. 'No one else believes my story. Only you. I'm a lonely woman, Mr Comber. There's no point pretending.'

Gerald doesn't say anything. He rummages around in his briefcase until his fingers touch a paper bag. He tears the bag open and removes the cake from its foil dish.

'Excuse fingers,' he says, placing it on the lid of her Tupperware box. 'Baked yesterday.' He hears her little gasp of pleasure and lifts the second pie, unseen, from its dish.

'Home cooking!' she says. 'It takes me back.'

They sit in silence. The pigeons swarm back, scratching

over the flagstones, their heads darting like little pistons as they race towards the crumbs. Gerald watches their beady, stupid eyes and dreams again of shooting them, one by one. He glances down into the open briefcase and notices that his UB40 has slipped from the pages of the thriller novel for the second time that morning.

'I'll miss our lunch-times together,' she says, finishing the tart and licking her lips extravagantly. A strand of hair blows across her face again and gets caught in the side of her mouth. This, too, she licks away. 'But everything's going to be all right now. I've been waiting a long time. . .' She closes her eyes again and smiles.

Mr Thaw crosses the forecourt and hurries up the steps. He's wearing red socks. He glances at the woman and he and Gerald exchange conspiratorial smiles. The breeze blows a spot of rain onto Gerald's cheek. Dark clouds are slipping across the sun; the windows of the shops over the road have turned a sickly yellow. His own windows might have to wait. . . The woman doesn't seem to have noticed: she looks as if she's fallen asleep.

There's the sound of someone shouting from the main entrance hall of the museum. Heads turn. The two security guards push themselves upright from the pillar and hurry inside. Better close the briefcase, or the book might get wet. He wants to get the windows cleaned before Monday morning at the latest.

He eats his breakfast at the living-room window every weekday morning and watches the commuter trains sliding into central London from the south. Six lines split and fan out acoss the waste ground. He can see it all from the thirteenth floor; and even in the winter, with the windows closed, he hears the wheels grating and humming over the rails, and that strange electric clicking as the trains slow down by the signal box. He never misses a morning – like he never misses a Saturday at the library. He sits down by the window at seven o'clock to catch the first commuter-filled trains, and he doesn't clear up the breakfast dishes until the lines become quiet after nine. Then, if the morning is dry, he cleans the windows. The view is the only thing he ever liked about the tiny flat.

There's something going on inside the museum. Gerald stands up. The woman is breathing heavily, her head on one side, the trace of a smile on her lips. He walks to the door. A small crowd has gathered in the recess beneath the main staircase. Gerald has never looked into the recess before, but now he can see the top of two doors in the back wall. Someone is shouting.

One of the security guards parts the crowd, and two men, flanked by more guards, are marched across the hall towards the security office. They look terrified. One of them is the man who reads *The Financial Times*. He glances at Gerald as they pass. Just for a second, Gerald imagines he sees a flicker of a smile pass over the man's face.

'We've been watching you,' one of the guards says, digging a gloved hand roughly into the man's ribs. 'We knew it was just a matter of time. You pervert!'

The door of the security room slams behind them, leaving the occupants of the museum hall whispering in tight, shocked little groups.

Gerald doesn't move for a while. He stands and stares at the polished mosaic floor. The damp air is blowing chilly against his back. Did he close his briefcase? He hopes she'll still be asleep. He wants to creep back to the bench, pick up his case and slip off without having to speak to her. The wind is swirling under the arches of the porch. A paper doily is dragged along the ground and tossed into the air above the steps. A police car stops outside the museum gates.

Gerald thinks about the two men now waiting in the security guards' office. The police are coming just for them. It couldn't have been a smile he'd seen as they'd passed by, and yet. . . He zips up his jacket and wonders if he'll ever have the courage to live even that much.

Easter

Good Friday, nine fifteen, and in the old market square a man in a white apron was scrubbing the flagstones outside his unlit café. The sound of his metal pail scraping against stone sent a flock of pigeons wheeling into the air, high above the central fountain. All the windows of the shops and cafés were dark, sunk in great slabs of shadow. Droplets of spray from the fountain sparkled against the granite trough, and the paving slabs at the centre of the square were already bathed in early sunlight. The pavements and the buildings remained, for the present, locked in pockets of shade.

Except for a few other café owners similarly engaged in preparing their premises for the busy day ahead, the square was quiet. The man swilled one last pail of soapy water across the flagstones and watched the bubbles explode silently. Then he set about arranging the red metal tables and chairs in front of the café. There were four chairs to each circular table – six tables in all. He glanced briefly up at the sky, and when he saw how blue it was, imagined he was back home. It wasn't often he looked at an English sky and thought of Italy; and when he did, he felt a shiver of regret.

A younger man on a bicycle appeared. He juddered across the uneven flagstones, finally stopping himself in front of the café by jamming his foot against the kerb.

'Business must be slack, Aldo, if you can stare into space at opening time!' The café owner smiled. The

47

young man's fair English skin looked unnaturally red that morning.

'And for you too, Mr Hartley, if you have time for sun-bathing!'

'On the contrary,' the younger man replied, stepping from his bicycle. 'Business is so good I was able to take the day off yesterday and go down to the coast.'

'And the café?'

'Chris doesn't need me around the whole time.'

'Ah,' the Italian said, nodding slowly, 'so it *is* you who has the last say in these matters. I always suspected so, despite what everyone else in the square has always said.'

Steve Hartley grinned at his rival.

'I can well imagine what everyone in the square has always said. I'm surprised at you listening to gossip. For your information, I left Chris fast asleep at home. It's his turn to have a holiday.'

'The sleeping partner, eh?'

'Something like that, Aldo.'

'So you have to work one of the busiest days of the season so far? It sounds as if Chris has done all right for himself.' The young man smiled again.

'But don't forget our new waiter, Eddy.'

'Ah yes,' Aldo said, 'the new waiter. He's also been talked about in the square.'

'I'm not surprised! He's bringing the girls flocking in. I bet you've all noticed a fall-off in business since he started at the Wildcat – not that you'd admit it, of course.'

Aldo gave a nonchalant shrug and smoothed his apron.

'I haven't noticed,' he said. 'But tell me: if this Eddy is so popular with the girls, why do you hope to make a favourable impression on him yourself?'

'I never said I did.' Steve gripped the handle-bars and prepared to move off.

Aldo smiled. 'You don't have to.'

'I suppose Maria is with you today?'

'Of course.'

'Of course. Look, I know Maria's been with you for twenty years and everything, but you really need to get some fresh blood in this place – someone like

Eddy.' Steve looked briefly towards the open café door. 'Otherwise, you're going to find yourself left behind by a new generation.'

'You think so?' Aldo said, as a young man with floppy fair hair and faded jeans sat down at a table.

'Hello!' Steve murmured.

'You see,' Aldo explained, 'good service is never out of fashion. Who else in the square is ready for the public? It's already past nine thirty and none of the other cafés is even unlocked. Now you must excuse me – I think we're in for a particularly busy day.'

With that, he slapped the younger man good-naturedly on the back and walked over to his customer.

'Am I too early?'

'Not at all,' Aldo assured the young man. 'We're just opening. What can I get you?'

'I'm meeting someone here, but I'm a bit early. I might as well have a cappuccino while I'm waiting. No hurry.'

'Certainly, sir.'

She looked at him and wondered if it was wrong to feel the way she did. The sensation was slight, but it was definitely there. She couldn't understand it. Nick had once told her that his friend was training to be a cabinet maker, and now, as the boy stirred his coffee, she noticed what beautiful hands he had.

'No thanks,' she said, as he offered her the stainless steel sugar bowl. 'I gave it up with nicotine a year ago.' She wondered what his fingers might feel like running down the side of her body. Cool, probably.

'I'm glad you and Nick stayed friends even when you weren't . . . together any more.'

He looked at her closely, and she felt uneasy. Some of Nick's other friends had glanced at her in a similar way at the funeral. They'd looked comfortable in black; almost professionally grief-stricken. As she'd left the little church, she'd noticed the funny way they looked at her – as if surprised at her composure. It seemed to her that they were waiting for her to break down. She knew they'd expected her to.

'There was no reason why we shouldn't have stayed friends,' the boy replied, pushing his hair away from his forehead. 'We still cared about each other. And I live close by, so we saw each other all the time.'

'I'll never forget finding you all there with him,' she said.

The strange thing was how she didn't seem really in control of what she felt or did. Now, just for a moment, she considered crying. The feeling lasted while she remembered Nick's flat; the sunshine flushing through the dirty living-room windows, the four strangers going about their tasks quietly and patiently, and the sharp, bird-like sound of breathing from beyond the bedroom door. She hadn't felt even a tinge of resentment. *She* wouldn't have known what to do. How could she have minded?

'It can't have been very easy having to cope with me,' she said. She respected him – him and the others in that tight, loyal little band of friends. She'd felt unhappy for them at the funeral, all of them in black, with their white faces and their red lips pushed stiffly down. She'd tried to explain to the priest when he'd touched her gently on the shoulder and told her how brave she was; but she'd known immediately that she'd confused him.

Aldo passed the table and smiled at them. 'Is everything all right?'

'Fine, thank you,' she replied.

Aldo found her very striking. It was unusual for British women in their middle years to be so stylish. As for the boy, well . . . he knew what Steve Hartley would say about him. Aldo was confused. Looking back at the couple from the dark café, he supposed it was just possible – but surely not. . .

She began to wonder if there might really be something wrong with her. Her son was dead. "Nick's dead, he's dead," she made herself think – the kind of deliberate thinking where she heard the words echoing in her head. The effort was pointless. The words rang hollow and empty around her brain and then just faded away. In those moments when the shock did come, it tore through her so violently she thought it must be visible to everyone. It was like being riddled with bullets, though even that was an inadequate description. When it was gone, it left her shaking a little.

They spoke for a few minutes about the flat. She said there were a few photographs she'd like to have; otherwise he should deal with Nick's belongings. She supposed Nick would have wanted that. It wasn't very likely that he'd saved any money. If there was anything, it should go to the support group. They'd even arranged the service. She hadn't much liked touching the stranger behind her, but the priest had asked them to do it, and she could see the point. It was funny thinking about it now, but at the time she'd felt angry. She'd turned back from the stranger – a girl with bad skin – and stared up at the coloured window in front of her. How dare they tell her what to do! Her son was dead – how could they? Thinking about it now was like recalling a stranger, and she felt foolish for having let herself be angry.

'Oh look! They're selling balloons.'

They stared across the square. A young man in a clown's outfit was manoeuvring a portable gas cylinder across the flagstones. From his left wrist, on taut strings, flew half a dozen inflated hearts made from silver plastic. They seemed fixed against the sky, scarcely moving except when the man jerked his arm and pulled them to one side or another. She imagined the bulging plastic bursting, the hearts drenching the clown in curls of thick, red blood.

'Have you spoken to Jill?' he asked.

'Yes, I spoke to her last night,' she replied. 'She's still upset at not being able to come over for the funeral, but it wasn't practical. She's due any day, and stress can sometimes bring it on. If she had come over, I'm sure she'd have gone into labour during the service, or something.'

She giggled. He decided she must be tired.

'Nick was always talking about her,' he said.

'Yes, they were very fond of one another.'

51

Poor Jill – always second best, and how she'd fought against that one! Over and over again she'd told herself that whatever else a mother did, she should never favour one child over another. It never seemed to be a matter of choice, though. It was an unalterable fact and all she could do was try not to let either of them notice. Peter had been as hopeless a father as he had been a husband, and the three of them had scarcely been able to conceal their gratitude when he'd left them for the solitude of a Welsh farm. The children had been young teenagers then, and though friends said what a bastard Peter was to leave them like that, it had been a huge relief to them all.

When Jill married an American airman from the local base and went off to the States, it could have been the end of the world, but her interest in Jill had never been really maternal. How similar would they turn out to be? Would she be beautiful? Would she want children? With Nick it had been different; but now he was dead she was beginning to wonder if even *he* had meant that much to her. Yes, she'd felt miserable, alone in her hotel room; but through her misery she'd still felt she was doing it all wrong.

The boy beckoned to the café owner, who hurried to their table, a round silver tray held like a discus at his side. They ordered two more cups of coffee.

'I don't want to keep you – I know it's your day off,' she said.

'I don't have anything to do this morning,' he said. 'It's nice just sitting here.'

She smoothed a crease in her skirt and remembered an afternoon twenty years earlier, when she'd sat in the launderette with her neighbour: two young mothers enjoying a few minutes of freedom. She couldn't think now where the children had been. She remembered confessing to her neighbour:

'I'm frightened of loving them too much,' she'd said. 'I'm afraid I'll be disappointed, like my mother was.'

She must have let out a quiet laugh at the memory, because when she looked up, he was smiling enquiringly at her.

'I'm sorry,' she said. 'I was just thinking.'

He smiled. 'I keep remembering things, too.'

'Of course you do.'

A group of tourists stopped outside the café and sat down at the next table. Shortly afterwards, an elderly couple sat down at another. The square was coming to life. On three sides, the pavement tables were gradually becoming occupied, and by the fountain a little group had gathered to buy the silver heart balloons and to feed the pigeons. Aldo's café was not the obvious choice for most people in search of refreshment, situated, as it was, on the side of the square that remained in the shade. The sun, though, was pushing ever nearer, in a long, straight line across the uneven flagstones, and was now within a few inches of the end tables. Somehow it didn't feel like Good Friday any more.

They talked about the support group. She said she couldn't help but feel involved: he told her the organisation placed great emphasis on parental involvement.

'It's the best way of educating the public,' he pointed out. She said she could see that. She wanted to lean across to the people at the next table and tell them what had happened:

'My son died last week. By the time I got to him, of course, he didn't look anything like he had last Christmas, but it was him – I recognised his smile. Now I have to learn new things, just when I thought I'd learned everything that interested me.'

She asked him if he was scared for himself. He said that generally he wasn't, but that sometimes he woke in a panic in the middle of the night. Electric light rationalised the fear away. At least he knew there were people around who would help if something happened.

No, she'd never forget arriving at his flat, watching all his friends quietly coping. She wondered if a real mother could have dealt with it. . .

Perhaps she'd sensed that one day she'd need to be detached. It meant that she didn't hate the young man opposite her. She could understand why her son had found him attractive. For a moment, she even imagined him and Nick lying naked together in bed. There was a lot to think about.

She had scarcely begun to think what Nick must have gone through worrying about what would happen when he became too weak to help himself, wondering how to tell her, deciding, apparently, that it was one difficulty too many. Now she realised just how much there was to learn; and the odd thing was, it felt exciting.

Steve Harley eased his way between the tables. He looked back at the blond boy before entering the café.

'He did love you, you know.'

'I know he did,' she replied. 'And I loved him – I really did. In my way.'

The boy nodded.

'He understood about that.'

She looked down and noticed that the tip of her shoe had pierced the straight line between shadow and sunlight. Glancing up again, she saw the boy looking past her, with an expression of vague amusement, towards the open door of the café.

'Well, I must go,' she said brightly. 'I still have to collect my suitcase and settle up at the hotel, and you know what trains are like on public holidays.' She stood up. 'Oh look!' she said, pointing towards the fountain. 'One of the silver hearts has escaped!'

Maureen

Vera skids on a pile of wet leaves by the factory gates. It's eight fifteen on a foggy morning, the last day of October. You can't see the playing fields beyond the railway cutting, or the line of poplars by the school building: you can't even see the far end of the trading estate. The hooter at the dairy sounds hollow and far off. The lights of the cars and lorries along Enterprise Way leave white streams in the fog. The air creeps up from behind and grabs you by the chest; it makes you cough. The pavement's full of people hurrying to work, hunched up in thick overcoats – everyone's coughing. It feels like winter.

She's too busy trying to recognise the muffled faces coming towards her to notice the pile of glistening leaves by the sweet factory gates. All she knows is that suddenly her feet are skidding forwards. There's nothing she can do but throw her left arm out, and that's not enough to stop her. A woman's voice cries out somewhere in the fog. Vera's hand crumples up on the tarmac and a sharp pain shoots through her wrist to her elbow.

Someone hurries up to her, brown suede boots thudding over the wet paving slabs.

'You all right, Vera? I saw you go down.'

'Ooh, the pain. . .'

'Hold on to me with your right arm, and we'll take you into the nurse. I hope nothing's broken – you went down with a real bang.'

'I'm done for. . .'

'Come on, now. I'll help you in. Can you stand?'

'Oh Maureen, you'll have to take charge today. I think I've broken my wrist.'

'Don't you worry about that. We'll take you in to the nurse and send you home.'

'Casualty! It's casualty I need!' The older woman sits on the pavement in her fur coat and wails above the noise of the traffic. 'Oh Maureen, it's a sign, I know it is – a *warning*! I'm too old to be doing this. It's time you took over. You can't be deputy for ever. I always said I'd bow out gracefully, and look how it's happened! It's my punishment for staying too long.'

'Rubbish,' Maureen says firmly. 'You've got years ahead of you. The factory couldn't run without you.' Yet as she speaks, a strange glow warms her right through; she can't explain it to herself. She lifts Vera. The old woman looks frail and helpless, but her right arm is like a vice round Maureen's waist, the uninjured hand grasping hard, like a claw.

This isn't what Maureen needs after a sleepless night. On the way to work she's been planning to tell Vera all about it – all about Rick and the other boy. She was going to tell her over morning coffee. She isn't sure she can trust Vera to keep quiet, but she knows she must talk to someone. They reach the factory door. Vera's eyes are full of tears. Two of the machine operatives watch from the gate and hold back, embarrassed.

'Let's get you inside,' Maureen says. 'Sit in reception. I'll go and find Rick. He left before me this morning – he'll be around somewhere. He can drive you to the hospital in one of the vans.'

It's warm in reception. Maureen notices the sweet, fruity smell for the first time in years. A tiny pocket of air escapes from her throat with a brief gurgle.

'Oh, that's better,' Vera says. 'It's nice and warm in here.' Three of the men from the cooking section clock on in the foyer.

'What's up, Vera?'

'Ooh, Pete!'

'Slipped and fell on her hand outside,' Maureen explains.

'You all right? You look very white.'

'It's the shock,' Maureen says.

'Oh, the pain!'

Pete calls through to the canteen: 'Eh, Vera's done her hand in slipping on the pavement!' There's a scraping of chairs in the canteen, and the women hurry in, their pink overalls crackling together in the crush.

'I'll go and find Rick,' Maureen says.

Everyone's watching Vera lying in her damp fur coat on the reception sofa. The canteen's empty, except for Dan. He's sitting by the radiator, reading a book. He doesn't notice Maureen, so she slips away from the open door as quietly as she can. She can't ask *him*.

Dan arrives on the factory floor to find he's been moved from the shrinkwrap to machine number thirteen – the noisiest of them all. When you sit on the platform watching the cutter chopping and shaping the toffee the machine vibrates till you think your fillings will fall out. Shirley's permanently on machine thirteen. In the canteen they'll tell you it's because of what she said to Vera after a vodka too many at the staff party last Christmas.

Shirley shrugs her shoulders when Dan arrives and looks towards the ceiling, as if to say 'Tough shit'. After nine months on number thirteen, she has a philosophical outlook on life. She slides off her seat and moves across to him. 'Got in Bat-face's bad books, then, have you?'

'Eh?' Machines are being started up all around him. He watches her mouth open and close.

'Vera moved you here as a punishment for something, then?' Shirley screams.

'No!' Dan shouts back. His throat already feels strained. 'Maureen's moved me this morning.'

Shirley nods, open-mouthed. A strand of hair has escaped from her white cap and is waving around in the air. She doesn't seem to have noticed and Dan wonders if he should tell her. He decides not to because of the effort it would take. He's felt like an outcast since his first day, when Vera introduced him in the canteen during morning break and described him as an 'intellectual'.

'Vera got 'er come-uppance this morning, then. . .'

'Eh?'

'I said, Spam-brain got taken down a peg or two – *this morning*!'

'Oh – yeah. Might have broken her wrist, apparently.'

'Didn't break her neck, worse luck,' Shirley screams, cheerfully. 'You 'aven't worked on thirteen before, 'ave you? Christine says it's better than a vibrator sitting here, but I don't s'pose you'll mind. . .' She narrows her eyes and winks. Dan decides he hasn't heard.

'We're doing the French order this morning. Mixed flavours, loose. So we're starting with lemon, all right?'

Dan nods and sits down by the cutter. His job is to make sure the workings don't get clogged up with toffee and to keep an eye on the cutter. The machines haven't been replaced since the factory was opened twenty years ago. Most of them break down twice a day, but machine thirteen usually manages to get jammed once every two hours.

The production office is above the factory floor and is reached by an iron staircase. It has a long glass window looking out across the factory. The procedure for dealing with breakdowns is simple. The machine operative stands on the platform facing the production office and screams as loudly as possible – 'Mau-reen!' Because of the noise of the surrounding machinery, most operatives wave their arms and make funny faces at the same time, to try and attract Maureen's attention. They've always turned to Maureen.

'Why'd they take you off shrinkwrap, then?'

'Eh?'

'Cushy on shrinkwrap – not that *I* ever got a turn with *her* around.' Shirley tosses her head in the vague direction of the supervisor's office, forgetting that Vera has been taken to hospital. 'The best I've 'ad is two months on number nine while Les was off with 'is dislocated shoulder.'

'Eh?'

'DISLOCATED SHOULDER!'

Dan nods. The stench of hot sweet strawberries is wafting in from the cooking room next door and mingling with the smell of machine oil. Shirley presses a switch and the roll of lemon wrapper starts to turn slowly on its spool above the machine. She watches it for a moment, making sure the paper isn't twisted. Then she nods and presses another switch which stops the spool moving.

Beneath the spool is a shallow metal dish, dusted with icing sugar. You push a slab of the toffee into the dish and it gets fed into the machine. It emerges in the middle as a long, square sausage. If you stand too close to the machine, the icing sugar gets up your nose and makes you sneeze. The cutter slices the toffee into little cubes which disappear back into the machine on a conveyor belt. They emerge in foil wrappers – a mouth-watering picture of the appropriate fruit on every one – and cascade like sparkling fireworks into big plastic trolleys.

Dan's never worked on the machine before, but Rick's explained it all to him. He sits and waits for the toffee to arrive from the cooking room. Shirley's gone off to chat to the woman on the next machine. Dan looks down to the far end of the factory, towards the stores and the rubber doors that flap open like huge elephant's ears when the forklift comes through with a pallet of paper or fruit concentrate. Rick isn't there. Dan can see Bernard through the window of the store manager's office. He must be eating something because his moustache is moving up and down.

The fog is still so thick you can't even see the line of conifers on the edge of the factory grounds, or the wall of the concrete yard where the lads from the laundry play football during the lunch hour. Most of the machines are now running, and only number thirteen has still to be switched on. The concrete floor is vibrating and the noise is ten times worse than at the shrinkwrap. Shirley's said something to the woman on the next machine, because they glance at Dan and giggle together. He scowls and turns away.

Rick's bringing a new roll of lemon wrapper to machine thirteen. Dan loves how his boots turn out when he walks, and the way his baggy overalls hide the shape of his body. Rick always has a smile and a joke for everyone but he's not smiling under his Chairman Mao cap this morning. He's keeping his eyes fixed towards the floor. He drops the roll of foil down by the platform. He can't resist just a quick look.

He looks tired, but the expression on his face gives nothing away as he glances first at Dan and then at Shirley. Most days he'd wait to hear Shirley's dirty joke, but this morning he just smiles a fleeting version of his funny, lopsided smile, and walks back towards the stores office. Shirley looks at Dan and shrugs her shoulders.

Dan turns away from her again. He doesn't care what she or the others think of him. In a week's time, he'll be sitting back in the gymnasium at the school he thought he'd left for ever. A few weeks after that he'll be gone. No more sitting in the sweet factory canteen during the dinner hour, trying to concentrate on history textbooks while the others play cards and smelly George from the cooking section makes comments about the queens of England. No more clocking on and clocking off, no more icing sugar tickling his nostrils, no more hot strawberry air sticking in his throat, no more walks to the bus stop at the end of the day with the sound of machine engines still ringing in his ears.

Big Pete from the cooking section arrives with a slab of yellow toffee curling slowly across his cradled arms. The tattoos on his forearms are dusty with icing sugar. He throws the toffee into the tray and contorts his face into something between a smile and a grimace. Dan watches him wipe his arm across the seat of his white overalls and stroll back towards the cooking section. Now Shirley's prodding the toffee down into the tray with her fist. Dan glances again towards the stores, and there's Rick, standing in the office talking to Bernard, but watching machine thirteen through the window. He looks unhappy.

Someone else is watching machine thirteen – from the window of the supervisor's office. Dan sees her when he turns to pick up the new roll of foil. They watch one another for a few moments. Neither of them notices the girl on the next machine until her screeching voice hollers above the roar of the machine engines:
    'Mau-reen!'

The fog lingers. It wraps itself around the factory walls and presses against the windows. There's a presentation for one of the cooks at dinner-time. He's getting married at the weekend and everyone congregates in the canteen. Maureen gives him an electric blanket and makes a short speech.

Dan doesn't want to watch. He turns his back on the assembled workers and stares at the fog through the window. He doesn't care about the dirty jokes from the machine operatives but the electric blanket in its polythene wrapper embarrasses him. There's nothing through the window, except the outline of the dairy wall, shrouded in white.

Maureen sits on Vera's orthopaedic chair while she waits for Dan. The chair bounces slightly whenever she moves. Now she's sitting in Vera's place, she can look over to her own desk. This is what Vera's seen all these years. She wonders who'll be the new deputy. Nothing's official yet, of course; but she's expecting a call from upstairs any time.

It's her chair now: her portable phone with built-in memory

function; her exclusive key to the filing cabinet; her seat on the monthly management liaison meetings. There's even a space marked out for her in the staff car park, somewhere under the stack of rusting desks by the boundary wall. She remembers a workman painting the words *Production Supervisor* on the tarmac twenty years ago. She's forgotten all about it until now; and she can't help smiling. She bounces a little harder on the chair and tells herself that this is her reward for years of waiting. She'd be in tears, only Dan's watching her nervously through the glass door.

He hasn't been this close to her before; but now he sees that Maureen's eyes are pale blue, just like Rick's. She tells him to sit down. The noise from the machines fades when she closes the door.

'Double glazing,' she says. 'Vera made them put it in.'

'I don't blame her.'

'Are you too hot?'

'No, I'm OK, thanks.'

'Vera has the outside windows covered with sheets of plastic every September. They take it away in April. We can't have the door open because of the noise. It gets stifling in here sometimes.'

Dan smiles and looks at his hands.

'I'm sorry I had to put you on thirteen.'

'That's all right. . .'

'Only there's three off with flu.'

'Yeah. . .'

'And what with Vera being off. . .'

'How is she?'

'She's fractured her wrist.'

Dan doesn't quite know what to say. 'Will she be coming back?'

'I don't think so. But don't say anything to anyone.'

'I won't.'

'I didn't think you would. You don't talk to many people here, do you?'

'Well. . .'

'I've noticed. It hasn't been easy for you to fit in.' She's

62

watching him closely. 'Has it – really?' A police van passes the factory, its siren wailing through the fog. Maureen doesn't take her eyes off him.

'I'm not getting at you,' she says. 'Only I've noticed it hasn't been easy for you. It's the same whenever we have students here working temporary. It makes the others nervous.' Dan's head starts to itch under his cap.

'They feel threatened. Do you understand?'

'Yes.'

'It makes them think of the things they might be missing – outside this place.'

'Yeah, I see what you mean.'

'But most of them are all right really.'

'Oh, I know. I get on all right with most of them.'

'You're leaving in a couple of weeks, aren't you?'

'A week on Friday. I've got my retakes next Thursday and Friday morning.'

'History, isn't it?'

'Yeah.'

'And then you're moving to London and working before you go to college next autumn?'

'That's right.'

'Rick said.'

Dan takes his cap off and scratches his head. His hair feels greasy. He lowers his hand and his fingers smell of strawberries. Maureen glances quickly down at the factory floor. 'Rick and I had a long talk last night,' she says.

'I know. He mentioned it at dinner-time.'

'You managed to speak to him, then? I didn't think you had. He's been avoiding both of us today. I noticed.'

'I saw him for a minute at the end of dinner.'

'You want him to go away with you to London.'

Dan doesn't say anything.

'It's all right,' she says. 'I know all about it. He told me everything last night.'

'Had you guessed?'

'Yes, I'd guessed.'

'I told him you had,' Dan says. 'But he was sure you hadn't.'

'I'm not stupid.'

'He didn't seem to know what you thought about it.'

'I don't really know myself. . .'

'We thought you'd go mad.'

Maureen smiles. 'He doesn't know me very well,' she says. 'You know he's sometimes spoken about joining the army? No, I see you don't.'

'He never mentioned it to me,' Dan says. 'Rick? In the army?'

'I don't know if he ever thought about it seriously. He first talked about it when he was still at school – and he's still here. He still mentions it sometimes, but I don't think he really means it.'

'What about him coming away with me?'

Maureen shrugs her shoulders. 'He seems to mean *that*.'

'But . . . aren't you angry? Or something?' He's not sure exactly what he wants to say.

Maureen gives a hard little laugh. 'Seems it's you or the army. What would any mother choose?'

Dan considers this for a moment. 'I should think most mothers would choose the army.'

'Do you think so?' She looks surprised.

'I'm sure they would,' Dan replies. 'I think *mine* would. At least if your son's in the army you can tell friends and relatives. And if he's blown to bits in Northern Ireland – well, at least you don't have to hide anything. There's no disgrace, is there?'

An alarm clock rings on the table. Maureen stands up and presses a buzzer on the wall which activates the break bell down on the factory floor. She watches the machinists hurry off to the canteen and then returns to her seat behind the desk.

'I suppose Rick told you about his father?'

'He said he went away when Rick was a baby. . .'

'Just took off one day. He was a carpenter. I got pregnant when I was eighteen and he married me because my father said he'd kill him otherwise. I often wonder why he didn't just go off then – just disappear and have done with it. Perhaps he thought my father would catch up with him, but when he *did* finally go, he made a pretty good job of it.'

'Did you try and find him?'

'I tried everything,' Maureen says. 'Though I didn't really want him back. I was doing it for the family mostly – my mother and father especially.'

'And you never heard anything from him?'

She shakes her head. 'I've been frightened of his turning up ever since,' she says. 'Because I think I'd have killed him.' She thinks about this and then says, 'Yes – I think I would. I just wish he'd gone off when it all started – when I got pregnant with Michael.'

'But then you wouldn't have had your other kids,' Dan points out. 'You wouldn't have had *Rick*.'

Maureen nods.

'But surely. . ?'

'Don't get me wrong,' Maureen says. She shrugs her shoulders. 'I love them. I mean, of course I do – I'm their *mother*. But if I hadn't had them, I could have done more with my life. That's what I'm saying. Don't get the wrong idea.'

'You wanted to be a nurse, didn't you? Rick said.'

Maureen laughs. 'He told you that, did he? I should've put that thought out of my head when I was still at school,' she says. 'No one ever told me what I had to do. It took me years to stop thinking about it. I just don't want to see Rick end up like me – doing what he thinks he should and not what he wants to. He's a lazy little sod, really. If he can get someone else to do his thinking for him, he will. I want him to go away because if he doesn't, I can see exactly what'll happen to him. It depresses me to think about it now – be even worse watching it happen for the next thirty years.'

She looks through the glass partition. Someone's waving up at her.

'I'm sorry,' she says. 'I'll have to go down. Twelve's stopped again. I'm sorry I can't talk more to you now, but there's a lot to do today with Vera and everything. . .'

'Yeah, that's all right.'

'Get him to bring you home one evening. It's too cold to stay outdoors.'

He grins at her, feeling embarrassed. 'Thanks.'

'I'm sorry, Rick,' she thinks, *'but I can't worry about you too.'*

Just as he's about to leave the room, he turns to her and says: 'Congratulations about the job.'

'Thanks,' she says. All in all, Rick thinks, she doesn't look too thrilled.

The fog is swirling under the yellow street lights along Enterprise Way. Dan breaks away from the other operatives at the factory gate. He manages to give them the slip without having to say goodnight and hurries along the pavement. He turns from the traffic onto a narrow path that runs past the playing field towards the railway line.

The path is dark and quiet. Few people use it now – not since a pensioner was mugged and beaten by the level-crossing gate. Dan remembers when it was just a gravel track with thick bushes on either side. The tarmac came when the hypermarket opened along Enterprise Way. The last bushes were ripped out after they found the dead man. They caught the two boys who did it. Dan saw their pictures in the local paper. He recognised them from junior school. They told the police they'd done it because they were bored.

Rick's waiting by the crossing as usual, with one foot up on the crossbar of the gate. He's smoking a cigarette and looking down at the rails. Dan wants to creep up, but his feet crunch over the frosty path and Rick turns round. He flicks his cigarette away. The glowing tip flies through the air and disappears in the fog.

'Hello.'

'Hello.'

Dan puts his arms round Rick, but Rick doesn't move, except to turn his face away a little.

'What's up?'

'Nothing.'

'Have you been waiting long?'

'About five minutes.' Rick sounds unhappy.

'It's all right!' Dan says. 'It's all getting sorted out. I spoke to your mum this afternoon. She called me into the office. She told me about your talk last night.'

'She'd guessed. . .'

'I know.'

'I knew she had.'

Dan laughs. 'Bit difficult keeping it secret when we're working in the same place.'

'S'pose so.'

'But she doesn't mind! She knows we want to go away and live together, and she doesn't mind!'

'She told you that?'

'Yeah – this afternoon! In the office.' Dan wants to hug his friend. He doesn't understand why Rick looks unhappy.

'She said the same to me at breakfast.'

'Well, that's all right then, isn't it? I don't know why we were so scared of her knowing. We can do what we want now. We can go to London at the weekend and look for somewhere to live.'

Rick lights another cigarette and holds the burning match between his fingers. It blackens and curls and goes out just before the flame reaches his skin.

'What's wrong?'

'I've been thinking,' Rick says. 'I don't think I want to go. . .'

Dan hears himself swallow. 'Why not?'

'I don't think I can leave, that's all. I don't think I'm right for living in London. It's too big. I've been here all my life. . .'

'So have I,' Dan says. 'And you wouldn't be alone. You'd have me.'

'I know, but. . .'

'Yesterday you said you wanted to go.'

'I know, but after I spoke to Mum last night I thought a lot about it,' Rick says. 'I've been thinking all day.'

'Is that why you've hardly spoken to me?'

'I've been down at the stores most of the day,' Rick says,

67

sounding irritated. 'I haven't had a chance. Anyway, it's not easy there. . .'

'You don't have to tell me! I know it isn't easy. . .'

They stand silently for a few moments. Neither knows what to say next. Metal doors slam somewhere along Enterprise Way. Music is playing in the school building at the far end of the fields.

'What's this about you joining the army?' Dan asks.

'What did she say?'

'She said you'd been thinking about joining the army. You never told me.'

'It was just an idea,' Rick says. 'I thought about it when I left school.'

'But Maureen says you're thinking about it now.'

'I'm not. I just make her think so sometimes, that's all.'

'That's not very kind. You must know it worries her.'

'That's why I do it,' Rick says, simply.

'I don't understand.'

Rick glances at him: it looks almost like a sneer. 'You don't have to.'

'But you still haven't told me why you don't want to come with me,' Dan says. 'Why've you changed your mind?'

Rick shrugs his shoulders and rubs the toe of his boot across the tarmac. 'Dunno.'

'But there must be *something*. There *must* be a reason.'

'I'm sorry, Dan. I just thought about it and changed my mind. What else can I tell you? Just one of those things. . .'

'What've I done wrong?'

'You haven't done anything wrong; don't be daft.' Rick paws at the tarmac some more. 'We're just different, that's all.'

The smell of burning leaves seeps across the railway through the fog. Dan wipes beads of chilly water from his eyebrows. It's pointless saying anything else – pointless *minding*, even; but he still wants to hug Rick, as they always do when they meet after work at the level crossing.

'Maureen says Vera probably won't come back,' Dan says.

Rick shakes his head. 'It's got too much for her,' he says. 'She was starting to make mistakes. Mum always covered for her. I told her she was daft. She deserves the supervisor's job after all this time. She deserves *something*. It's her reward – what she's wanted for ages.'

'Is it?'

'Yeah, but she's never said. She's like that, my mum; you never know. . .'

'I like her. . . She was nice to me when I went in to see her this afternoon.'

Rick won't look Dan in the face. He's staring across the railway tracks towards the playing fields and the faint smudges of light, far in the distance, from the school building.

'I'll think about you next Friday morning,' he says, still not looking. 'Honest.'

'Thanks.'

'You'll do it easy. No problems.'

'I'll have to, won't I?' Dan shifts his weight. He's scarcely thought about the exam for weeks. It's starting to feel cold. The tarmac under the level-crossing light is shining with specks of frost. Further along the track a signal drops with a dull, metallic clunk.

'I'm sorry, Dan, but how can I go? You understand, don't you? I do like you, and everything, but . . . I'm frightened, I s'pose.'

There's a faint whipping noise on the rails and another clunk somewhere along the track towards the town. Rick has turned away from the gate, anxious to be away. A train hooter sounds, far off near the by-pass flyover.

'I've got to go now. I told Mum I'd be in by six.' He sounds like a little boy.

Dan blows a stream of breath towards the gate and joins Rick on the path. They look at each other. Dan shrugs his shoulders and smiles.

'Listen, it's all right,' he says. 'It was just an idea.' And Rick smiles uncertainly as the last train of the day slides past the level crossing towards the station.

Realia

Barnie pulled down his jeans and boxer shorts and leaned over the bench.

'Is this your first time?' the man said.

'Yes.'

'It's not as bad as you expect it'll be.' It was an efficient voice. 'The best way is to stick it in before you know it, and then. . .'

Barnie cried out. Something that felt like an aluminium drinking straw was chiselling deep into his flesh. His fingers grabbed at the sheet of green kitchen paper on the bench. He watched his fingers clench and stretch like claws; then he buried his face in the paper. It smelt of Dettol.

'. . . it's over before you know it. Keep still.'

He could feel something cold being wiped across his left buttock.

'I'll put a plaster on it. Keep still for a few moments.'

'I'm sorry,' Barnie said, 'I've spoilt your paper.'

The man laughed. 'Don't have to worry about that.' Barnie heard him ripping the plastic strips off a piece of plaster, and then his hand, pressing into the flesh at the top of his buttock again.

'. . . not that it's bleeding,' he heard him say. 'You can stand up now, but take it slowly. Some people react very quickly.'

Barnie turned round. The man removed his latex gloves and dropped them neatly into a bin. Then he walked over to the bench and screwed up the sheet of paper.

'Sit down,' he said, gesturing towards a chair by the desk.

'I'd rather not, thanks.'

'It probably won't hurt now – it'll be later on you'll feel it in the muscle. I should take it easy tonight if you can.'

'It's a bit difficult,' Barnie said, 'I'm supposed to be helping supervise a football match between two language schools.'

'You're not thinking of *playing*, I hope,' the doctor said, looking surprised.

Barnie laughed at the idea. 'God, no! We're leaving that to the students.'

'Good. I wouldn't advise anything too strenuous. Try not to be too late to bed, either.'

'What's going to happen to me?'

'Oh, it's hard to tell,' the doctor said, reassuringly. 'You might experience dizziness and nausea. On the other hand, you might not have any reaction to it at all. It varies from person to person.'

Barnie looked worried.

'But it won't be too awful, whatever happens,' the doctor continued, smiling for the first time. 'You'll be as right as rain in no time.'

Barnie sniggered. It sounded a ridiculous expression from someone in a white coat.

'Now you've had a word with Mrs Deacon, the social worker, haven't you?'

'Yes,' Barnie said. 'I wasn't very helpful, I'm afraid.'

'We would like to follow up your contacts.'

'So would I.' A fleeting image of the French coach driver swam into Barnie's mind. A hot afternoon, and the sun beating through the windscreen – the smell of hot plastic from the vinyl anti-macassars as they made their way to the back of the coach and pulled the curtains across the windows – Barnie watching the back of the man's head; the oily black hair hanging in curls on his sun-burned neck – a fleeting glimpse of another driver pissing against a fence as they closed the last curtain and hid from the coach park.

'I believe you think it was a *casual* contact. Am I right?' Barnie nodded. 'Someone I met when I was up in London a few weeks ago. I'm afraid I've no idea how to contact him, except through an appeal on French television.'

'Well, I don't think we need to go that far,' the man said, scribbling something on a piece of paper. 'Have there been any other casual contacts?'

'No,' Barnie said, truthfully. 'None for ages.'

'Well, that simplifies matters.' The man drummed his fingers on the table top. 'Now the only problem, I gather from Mrs Deacon, is telling your partner. Am I right?'

Barnie didn't say anything.

'I am right, aren't I? You are in a permanent relationship?'

The shock of hearing that was worse than two point four million units of penicillin G benzathine coursing into his body. He tasted Dettol on his lips; then he passed out on the chair.

Hilary was wearing a pale blue tracksuit and carrying a sports bag across one shoulder. Barnie watched her approaching across the grass; at first a smudge of blue and orange on the path near the river, then progressively clearer, until he could see her cheeks flushed red after her long walk and her ginger hair waving in untidy curls round her head. She collapsed, gasping, on the bench beside him.

'Jesus! I thought I'd be the last one! Where *are* they?'

The park was deserted, except for a few people exercising their dogs and a small group of teenagers playing with a Frisbee by the bandstand.

'I don't know,' Barnie said. 'I got here fifteen minutes ago. I thought I'd got the wrong place till I spotted you.'

They scanned the park. It was eight o'clock, the end of a scorching July afternoon. The sun was sinking behind great fingers of pink cloud above the boathouse roofs.

The first traces of mist were blurring the railings of the foot-bridge at the far end of the park, where the river wound between streets of solid Edwardian villas. The air was growing cooler. The sound of disco music and laughter wafted across the park from the pub on the river bank.

The lights in the beer-garden trees waved and sparkled in the breeze.

'I bet they're over there,' Hilary said. 'It's going to be too dark to see anything soon. I don't know why we bother to try and arrange anything.'

'If we didn't, someone'd complain to Charlotte,' Barnie said.

'We'll give them five minutes,' Hilary said decisively, 'and then we'll go over to the pub. I *bet* they're over there.'

'Did you phone Charlotte?'

Hilary groaned and pulled a sweater out of her bag. 'She wasn't there. I spoke to a secretary who promised she'd phone me back before seven. I left at twenty to eight, and nobody'd phoned.'

'Cow!'

'I left a message. I said to tell Charlotte that we'd run out of paper; we were having trouble with other language schools using our rooms and that the course books they sent up are crap.' She pulled the ring from a can. 'D'you want a sip of Vimto?'

'Pass,' Barnie said.

'I hardly had time to eat my tea,' Hilary said. 'I spent the whole afternoon marking the test papers.'

'How are they?'

'Lousy. And then I had to get my lesson plans done for tomorrow. That took me bloody hours.'

'It's hopeless.'

'If the money wasn't better, I'd be tempted to go back to the knicker-packer factory. At least you could forget about it at the end of the day.'

'I can't understand what's happened to the tutor from the other school,' Barnie said. 'I thought he was really keen on all this.'

Hilary wiped her mouth with the back of her hand. 'He was when I suggested it,' she said. '*Nigel.*' She made a face.

'*Nigel!*' Barnie echoed. They laughed.

'Might have known,' Hilary said. 'Chinless bloody wonder!' She stood up and scanned the park again.

'Well, they're not coming, are they? Shall we go over to the pub?'

'Might as well.'

'I *bet* they'll be over there.'

'How was Ingeborg this morning?'

Hilary groaned again. 'Bloody Ingeborg! Came in wearing a vest so small everything was falling out – *that* didn't help Adolpho's concentration. And then I made the mistake of handing out a *Daily Mail* article about the Olympics.'

Barnie frowned.

'Yes, I know,' Hilary said. 'That set her off again, telling us all, for the ninetieth time, how she's ranked number three among Finland's women water-skiers.'

'Jesus!'

'She came to the front of the class and gave us a demonstration of how you stand when you're water-skiing.'

'How *do* you stand when you're water-skiing?'

'Sort of bent over,' Hilary said. 'Adolpho was beside himself. I nearly had to send him out of the class. We hardly got a scrap of work done. How were the twins?'

'Heavenly as ever. Misha arrived on a bicycle. He wouldn't say where he'd got it.'

'Don't tell me they're turning to crime now.'

'Well, it didn't look like a hired number to me,' Barnie said.

They left the tarmac path and stepped onto the grass, already damp with evening dew. The noise of music and laughter grew louder as they approached the pub.

'That's the last thing we want – students being arrested for petty theft. That'll hammer the last nails in our coffin if Charlotte finds out.'

'I suppose I should have made more of an effort to find out where he'd got it,' Barnie said. 'I was just surprised he'd even turned up.'

'What was the class like?'

'All right. They complained about it being too hot. I tried to get them interested in that piece on Stratford from the tourist board brochure. . .'

'Getting them ready for the weekend?'

'That was the idea. I should've known better. They were much more interested in Alton Towers theme park.'

'I'd much rather spend next Saturday at Alton Towers than Stratford,' Hilary said.

'So would they.'

'Why don't we. . .'

'No!' Barnie said. 'They'd be throwing up all over the coach on the way home and you can bet Charlotte would find out. Anyway, she's already booked the coach.'

They trudged across the grass in the fading light and pondered the forthcoming day trip.

'And Jas would be disappointed,' Barnie said. 'He's looking forward to taking charge and doing the guided tour bit.'

'He's really serious about that?' Hilary said.

'Damn right he's serious.'

'So we can have an easy time?'

Barnie sighed. 'Well, Jas is sure to know more than I do. He always does.'

'Are you going to tell them who he is?'

'You're joking, aren't you? Even my English isn't good enough to describe Jas and our relationship. It's had me stuck for words for months. By the way, what's the subjunctive?'

They were nearly at the pub.

'The what?'

'The subjunctive. Antonella mentioned it this afternoon. She wants us to cover it one lesson.'

Hilary looked at him, horrified.

'You should put a stop to that,' she said. 'You can't have students asking to do things. You don't know *where* it could lead. Especially if they ask for something difficult like the subjunctive.'

'Is it difficult?'

'I read about it in a book once,' Hilary said. 'It looks very difficult. Just tell her it's archaic.'

'But what *is* it?'

'It's things like "Were she to go to the supermarket, she wouldn't have enough money".'

'Oh,' Barnie said.

They joined the path that led to the pub.

'Isn't that Ingeborg up that tree?' said Hilary.

Barnie couldn't get comfortable in bed. It hurt to lie down on his back, and if he lay on his right buttock, it meant facing Jas. *He* was drinking Bovril from a pint mug. He did it every night when he was reading. He kept a packet of French toast on the bedside table and regularly dunked half a dozen into his drink. The routine never varied, unless they'd had a particularly late dinner party, because Jas was a creature of habit. He said it reminded him of the nursery.

Barnie watched him finish the last of the French toast and screw the empty packet into a ball while he carried on reading.

'What are you reading?'

'Hmm?' Jas turned the page.

'What's the book?'

'A guide to Warwickshire.'

'I thought you were reading another Waverley novel.'

'I am,' Jas said, 'but I thought I ought to gen up a bit on Stratford. I don't suppose you have.' He didn't take his eyes from the book.

'I've been busy,' Barnie said. 'I've had a hard afternoon in the classroom.'

'I wish you'd keep still. What's wrong with you this evening?'

'I can't get comfortable.'

'God knows what you'll be like if you ever get a real, full-time job,' Jas said, flicking over another page. Barnie watched him.

'Why are you looking at me?'

'Christ, what's got you? I'm only looking,' Barnie said. 'And I'm lucky to have any job at all. We're not all fortunate enough to have finished our education twelve years ago. In those days you had something called choice.'

'So why are you complaining about having a job?'

'I'm not complaining.'

'Yes, you are.'

'No, I'm not.'

Jas sighed and settled down under the duvet, turning slightly away from Barnie.

'Anyway,' Barnie said, 'did you have a good day at the office?'

'Hmm.'

He looked round the bedroom. Jas had folded his trousers and shirt neatly on the chair by the wardrobe. There was an arrangement of dried flowers in the fireplace that Barnie hadn't noticed before. He wondered if he should ask Jas about it. On the mantelpiece was the photo of Jas's parents leaving an embassy dinner in Hong Kong and a more recent picture of his sister taken on graduation day at Oxford. In two years, Barnie had never met the family. Jas's parents had visited one day, six months or so after Barnie had moved in. All of Barnie's things had been squeezed into the spare bedroom the night before, jammed among the pieces of furniture Jas was keeping for when he bought a house. They'd stayed there ever since, because Jas thought it would be nice for Barnie to feel he had his own room.

Barnie hated the smell of Bovril at the best of times, but tonight it was making him feel sick. He wondered what the reaction would be if he threw up over the carpet or the duvet. Presumably Jas would notice. . . In the kitchen, the washing machine finished spinning six white shirts and shuddered to a stop. Jas put the book down and got out of bed.

'Do you want a drink of water?' he asked.

'Yes, please.'

Jas was wearing a pair of white shorts and a vest. Barnie watched him disappear from the bedroom and tried to remember when he'd last slept with no clothes on. Should he tell him the news when he came back with the water? Would reading about Stratford or seeing his clean white shirts tumble from the front loader have made him more potentially prepared for bad news? Barnie chewed a finger nail and pulled the duvet up to his neck. He suddenly felt scared. He couldn't see anything comforting when he looked round the room.

'I was just looking at the hall,' Jas said, returning with a mug of water.

'Were you?' Barnie said.

'It needs painting, but I don't know if there's any point.'

'Why?'

'Well, if I *did* buy somewhere. . .'

'Oh yeah. . .'

Jas looked at him suddenly. 'Barnie, are you all right?'

'Yes, I'm all right. Why?'

'What are you doing hiding under the duvet like that?'

'I'm not hiding!' Barnie laughed and reached for the mug.

Jas got back into bed. Barnie had moved slightly, so there was no danger of them touching.

'Well, if I've decided not to buy by September,' Jas said, settling down, 'I suppose I'd leave it until the spring. I could decorate the hall then.'

'Yeah.'

Jas picked up his guide book and began reading again. A strange sensation, somewhere between an ache and a dull pain was rippling through Barnie's left buttock, but he didn't dare move again. Jas looked absorbed in his book: it didn't seem the right time to say anything.

He turned slowly onto his side and picked up a thick paperback from the bedside table. His nose filled with tiny particles of dust as he flicked through the pages. He found what he was looking for on page five hundred and eighty. It read:

"The subjunctive is the name of a special group of verb forms which are used in a few cases to talk about events which are not certain to happen – which we hope will happen, or imagine might happen, or want to happen".

He stared at the sentence for a few moments, re-reading it several times. He wished it were the end of the year. Jas would have bought a house or painted the hall by then. He wondered where *he'd* be. Something would have been resolved, one way or another. He let the book fall to the floor and closed his eyes.

The weather grew hotter and the students less attentive as the week drew to a close. Barnie cycled into the church hall car park on Friday morning to find Hilary waiting outside for him. She looked worried. A few students were milling around outside the main door. Most of them were drinking cans of coke or fizzy orange. The twins were munching burgers by the bicycle rack. One of them was clutching what looked like a roll of five-pound notes. They turned towards the wall when they saw Barnie arrive.

'I've got terrible news,' Hilary said. 'I feel sick.'

'Oh dear,' Barnie said. 'Well, cancel the lesson. They won't mind a morning off.' Then he added, half-heartedly: 'Or I'll help you out with the group. . .'

Hilary shook her head. 'That's not the bad news,' she said. 'It's the news that's made me feel sick. The caretaker's just had a phone call from Charlotte.'

'At this time of the morning?'

'The woman's a fanatic,' Hilary explained. 'She told him to tell me she's coming on the trip tomorrow.'

'You're joking!'

'Watch me roll around the car park.'

'Oh, Christ!'

'She's travelling from London and meeting our coach when it gets in. She wants to see our lesson plans for the past four weeks and hear what we've been doing.'

'Fuck me!'

'It gets worse,' Hilary said, lighting a cigarette. 'She plans to come back with us, and we've got to arrange some kind of party for the students, here in the evening!'

Barnie sniggered nervously.

'The caretaker's furious. He says he won't be here to lock up. They had a real row over the phone, he says, but she told him it was in the agreement she signed with the church.'

'What sort of party?'

'She wants games and jelly and stuff like that.'

'For *this* lot?' Barnie said. 'We've got a sex-mad water-skier, a pair of thirteen-year-old twins who look like they're turning into Yugoslavia's answer to the Krays, a fifty-eight-year-old nuclear physicist and twenty or so adolescents who just want to go shopping. What does she think this is?'

'If she'd taken the trouble to come down and see us before, she'd know better,' Hilary said.

'Well, I hope you're going to phone her back.'

'Of course I am,' Hilary said. 'But she'll be in a meeting, or teaching Japanese businessmen or something. You know what she's like – she's *never* there when you want to talk to her.'

Three of the girls passed them. One of them was swinging a Harrods bag.

'Where were you yesterday, Antonella?' Hilary asked her.

'I was in London – shopping,' the girl replied, good-naturedly. 'Harrods, Selfridge, Katharine Hamnett.' She smiled at them and went off to find her friends.

'I sometimes think life's passing me by,' Hilary said, rubbing her eyes wearily.

Hilary got through to Charlotte during morning break. Her 10p lasted just long enough for Charlotte to tell her there was no going back on the plan: she was meeting them at Stratford and returning on the coach for the party. She'd already booked herself into the Garden House Hotel. Was there anything else Hilary wanted to discuss?

Barnie broke off writing up his lesson plans and cycled off to Sainsbury's to buy jellies and ice cream. On the way back to the flat he stopped off at the University bookshop and searched in vain for a book of party games. The shop assistant advised him to try the news kiosk on the station.

Back at the flat he loaded the ice cream into the freezer, cramming the tubs between packets of *petit pois* and frozen puff pastry. Then he stripped off his clothes and ran a bath. The flat seemed funny when Jas wasn't there. It felt as if he were walking through a show house. There wasn't a speck of dust anywhere. He lay in the bath and listened to the hum of the immersion heater. The ache in his left buttock had gone completely now. So much of his time had been taken up with the summer school, he'd scarcely thought about his visit to the clinic the previous Monday afternoon, and the pain he'd felt when the needle had gone in.

He tried to visualise a map of Italy with his eyes closed. Then he dressed in a clean white t-shirt, fresh socks and a clean pair of jeans and went into the kitchen in search of something to eat. He felt neat and tidy, like everything in the flat.

The coach journey to Stratford was one of the most uncomfortable Barnie had ever known. They pulled out of the church hall car park shortly after nine forty, delayed by ten minutes because the twins turned up late. Already the sun was baking the dusty fabric on the backs of the seats and there was a bitter smell of stale cigarettes.

The twins eventually arrived, carrying a massive holdall between them. It contained a picnic which included pâté and madeira cake from Harrods. Hilary wanted to know how they'd got hold of them. The twins gazed endearingly at her and then at one another, and pretended they didn't understand. Hilary made them sit near the front of the coach so she could keep an eye on them.

'They've been *shoplifting* in Harrods!' she whispered to Barnie as she sat down.

'They can't have been,' Barnie said. 'They haven't been to London.'

'Well, they must have bribed Antonella to steal them, then.'

'That is a very serious allegation,' a voice said from across the aisle. It was Ingeborg. She removed her sunglasses and gave them a chilling smile. 'I couldn't help hearing what you said.' A copy of *Elle* slipped from her lap and hit the floor with a sleek smack. Jas leaned across and picked it up.

'Thank you,' she said. 'You're very kind.'

Jas smiled at her.

'I didn't mean it as you probably interpreted it,' Hilary said. 'Probably. . .'

'You have to understand,' Ingeborg said, 'that they come

from a wealthy family in Yugoslavia. Their country isn't at all like people often assume it to be. Of course, I've travelled quite extensively across Europe, with the Finnish water-skiing team, and so I feel I've gained a *per-spective*.' She pronounced the last word very carefully. 'The twins' family are very . . . er . . . well-done back in Yugoslavia, I think.'

'Well-to-do,' Jas said, helpfully.

'Thank you!' Ingeborg said, flashing him a broad smile. 'I practise my English conversation for two hours every evening with my landlady.'

'Jesus!' Barnie hissed. 'We haven't even reached the motorway yet.'

'I dreamt about the knicker-packer factory last night,' Hilary said, gazing through the window. 'Everything was glowing. I thought it was heaven.'

'I don't think we've been introduced,' Ingeborg said. 'You're our guide, hmm?'

Jas shifted from his seat in front of them and went to join her. From the back of the coach came the unmistakable sound of a cork popping, followed by laughter.

'Hila-ree!' someone shouted. 'Bobo wants the toilet!'

A hand touched Barnie's shoulder. It was Vera, the Yugoslav nuclear physicist. She was dressed in a white trouser suit.

'You should know,' she said, 'that one of the Italian boys is distributing pornography. I am quite shocking.'

Ingeborg giggled loudly at something Jas said.

Charlotte was waiting at the car park just off the main street. She stood by the door and handed out street maps of Stratford. She instructed everyone, child and adult alike, in the same efficient voice, to form a neat semi-circle by the rear wheel. It was the first time Barnie had seen her. She was everything he'd visualised during their brief telephone conversations. A heavily-built woman of around forty, she was wearing a blue floral dress with lace at the collar and cuffs, and white sandals with a matching leather shoulder-bag. Her hair was frizzy and vaguely red. She had too much face powder on her cheeks. There was a white suitcase on the tarmac beside her.

Barnie clambered down the steps from the coach and introduced himself.

'Stand here a minute, would you?' she said. 'I'd like a word with you and Hilary.' She gave him a street map, but she didn't smile.

'Hello, Hilary. I thought you'd never get here.' She smiled briefly as Hilary emerged from the coach.

'Are we late?' Hilary asked, blinking in the strong sunlight.

'You are, rather.'

'This is Jas,' Hilary explained, as Jas emerged, closely followed by Ingeborg. 'He's helping out as a guide. He's been here before.'

'Hello,' Jas said.

Another brief smile rippled across Charlotte's face.

'Well, I'm glad you've come,' she said. She turned and looked at Barnie. 'I believe *you've* never been here before.'

'No, I haven't.'

'Extraordinary!' Charlotte said, expressionless.

'I thought so, too,' Jas added. 'I couldn't believe he'd never been here before.'

'Well, that's the generation gap for you,' Barnie said, staring coldly at Jas.

'So, I count nineteen without the three of you,' Charlotte said. 'Why hasn't everyone come?'

'Three of the girls went shopping in London,' Hilary explained.

'But this is part of the course, Hilary. Didn't you explain that?'

'I told them they were expected to go,' Hilary said. 'But they said they weren't coming.'

'Just like that?' Charlotte said, a look of disbelief on her face.

'I'm sorry, Charlotte,' Hilary said. 'I couldn't physically drag them onto the bus. Two of them are bigger than me.'

Charlotte looked at the group of students for a moment and then called up to the coach driver: 'I've got an overnight bag. Can I put it in the luggage locker?'

83

'Leave it by the door at the side, luv,' the driver called back. 'I'll stick it in for you.'

'Charming!' she hissed.

'Here, let me help you with it,' Jas said, picking up the suitcase.

'Thank you!' It was the first time she'd smiled properly. 'I'd like a word with you both,' she said again, glancing quickly at Hilary and Barnie.

It was decided that Jas would take the group on a short guided tour of the town, stopping by the river where they could eat their packed lunches. Charlotte explained to Jas that she wanted to go off and have a word with Hilary and Barnie about how things were going. Jas said he quite understood. Barnie heard Charlotte tell him that, frankly, it was a relief to find someone responsible and mature and willing to take charge. Then he half-heard her say something about being disappointed. Jas gave the game away by glancing towards the coach door. Hilary didn't notice, but Barnie glared for a second time. It wasn't turning out the way he'd hoped. He'd decided, earlier in the week, that today might be a good opportunity to talk to Jas. He knew it was cowardly, choosing a time when they were with lots of other people, but there didn't seem to be any chance of them talking properly at home. There just never seemed any motivation, on either side, to discuss anything.

When the driver had put the suitcase in the luggage hold, Charlotte stood in front of the wheel and lectured the students. She seemed not to have noticed that among them was a woman of fifty-nine and two men who could only have been ten years – if that – her junior. Hilary and Barnie stood by the door and cringed. At one point Ingeborg looked across at them in amazement. Barnie, not caring much, shrugged his shoulders helplessly.

The straggling group, led by Jas and Ingeborg, set off across the car park towards the town centre. Charlotte turned to Hilary and said: 'I think perhaps a cup of tea somewhere, don't you? I hope you've both brought your lesson plans and what have you. I want to see the kind of thing you've been doing with the students. None of them seemed to have much to say for themselves.'

'I think. . .' Barnie began.

'Your friend is charming,' Charlotte continued, cutting him off. 'I'm sure *he'll* make the trip worthwhile. After all, it is supposed to be an educational trip – as you'll see if you look at our brochure.'

They went to a café overlooking the river, where they sat on a wooden verandah at a table with a plastic cloth. A waitress came out and took their order.

'Tea for three I think, don't you?' Charlotte said.

'I'll have a coke, thanks,' Hilary said.

'And for me.'

'Terrible for the figure.'

'I don't think Hilary and I have to worry about that,' Barnie said, smiling sweetly. The waitress hurried away. She had enough to do without getting involved in any row.

Charlotte didn't waste any time.

'I must say to both of you,' she said, turning her sunglasses case in her hands, 'I'm a *little* concerned by the way things are going generally in Cambridge.'

Barnie wanted to ask her how she knew, since she hadn't been up to see them since the course had started.

'Now I employed you, Barnie, on the strength of your CV and two telephone conversations. I know you've done the RSA course, and I usually consider myself a good judge of character – I hope I haven't made a mistake.'

'I'm sorry, Charlotte,' Barnie said, 'I'm not with you.'

'Well, Hilary has phoned me on . . . quite a few occasions.'

'But I never complained about Barnie,' Hilary said quickly. 'I said he was doing well.'

'I'm not talking just about Barnie, Hilary. I'm talking about the general way the course is going. It's just that sometimes I've wondered if you couldn't sort out some of the "problems" yourself – without phoning me every five minutes.'

'Every five minutes?' Hilary looked furious. The waitress returned, deposited cups and glasses on the table and hurried away.

'Now don't get all defensive, Hilary,' Charlotte said, dunking the tea-bag in her cup by its string. 'This is constructive criticism. We all have to learn. After all, I was new to the job once, and look at me: I own my own school.'

'I'm sorry,' Hilary said, 'but I haven't phoned you every five minutes. We were put in a church hall that was double-booked with another language school; we haven't had enough course books, and the ones we have had aren't very good; and I wasn't given enough expenses money. I've *had* to ring you to find out what we're supposed to do.'

'But Hilary,' Charlotte said, with a sickly smile, 'when you came for your interview in London, you seemed a resourceful, level-headed girl who could take the initiative in things. That's precisely why I employed you. I explained that you'd be on your own more than usual because we're based in London. It's the first time we've had a summer school in Cambridge. The Oxford one goes like clockwork every summer. I'm wondering why you seem to have had these apparent difficulties.'

Hilary looked across at Barnie for support.

'We just thought you might come down occasionally to see us,' Barnie said.

'Especially at the beginning,' Hilary added.

'But as I've just said,' Charlotte continued, 'I run the school back in London. Apart from the responsibilities I have as the owner, I'm the senior tutor. I can't be dashing off to hold people's hands and pat them on the shoulder all the time.'

Barnie looked at her hands. They were still fiddling with the glasses case. Her carefully manicured fingernails were the colour of dirty blood.

'Anyway,' she continued, 'we'll go through your complaints one by one and try to sort them out. I told Jas – is it Jas? Unusual name – I told Jas we'd meet up by the theatre at one o'clock. I'll have to leave you for a short time. There's a few things I need to buy. We have to be back at the coach for two thirty, for Anne Hathaway's cottage. I hope Jas is coming to the party this evening. He seems very interesting.'

Charlotte looked through Hilary's lesson plans first. She nodded approvingly from time to time and even laughed once.

'That's an old favourite,' she said, pointing at something. 'It never fails.' She handed them back to Hilary with a smile. Her expression changed when she looked through Barnie's papers. Once she even tutted loudly.

'Anything wrong?' Barnie asked, bracing himself.

'Wrong?' she replied, looking up at him. 'Where's the spark, Barnie? Where's the *oomph*?'

'The what?'

'It's all so *dry*.'

'Is it?'

'Well, look. I mean, where's your realia for one thing?'

'Sorry?'

'Your *realia*. Surely they taught you about that on the course? Your *things*. Your empty washing-up bottles, your railway timetables, your mixed veg.'

'Mixed veg?'

'You can't stand in front of a classroom with just the blackboard to get you through. You're going to send the students to sleep.'

'But there wasn't time for all that,' Barnie said.

Charlotte looked at him. 'But what were you doing?'

'I was teaching,' Barnie said. 'What was I supposed to do? Drag them round Tesco's every afternoon?'

'I'm sorry, Barnie. I can't help wondering if you've really got it in you.'

'Thank you.'

'Well, it's got to be said. Don't you understand? *Things* are important. People relate to them – it's life, isn't it? How can you expect to get important ideas across by talking about them and writing them down?'

'Well, that's how I learnt when I was at school,' Barnie

said. 'You're saying nothing has any relevance unless it can be quantified in objects.'

Charlotte shook her head. 'You have to find the liveliest, most stimulating way of getting the complexities of language across,' Charlotte said. 'A language teacher is like a magician – always ready to pull a new surprise from the hat.'

'Like a stick of celery?' Barnie suggested.

'Possibly, yes. Most of the time you're dealing with people who don't really want to be there. Incorporating realia in your lessons makes them more receptive. Look at your group, for example. I bet they come into the classroom with carrier bags full of things: Walkmans, books, make-up, magazines, different bits of food and drink. You should work your way into the lesson – especially if it's something difficult you've got to get across – by using those things. Don't you see what I mean?'

Barnie was thinking about Jas. 'Yes,' he said.

'It looks like it's all here, more or less,' Charlotte said. 'I'm not criticising the teaching content of the lessons. It just lacks the spark. Try it.'

'I will,' Barnie said.

When she'd gone off to the shops, Barnie and Hilary wandered across to the river bank. Barnie looked into the brown water and said: 'I feel a bit guilty. I wonder if I'm being chauvinistic about her. Am I expressing the typical male fear of the powerful woman?'

Hilary glanced at him dubiously.

'I mean, from another woman's perspective, what do you think of her?'

'She makes my flesh crawl,' Hilary said. 'D'you wanna can of Vimto?'

They lay back on the grass and talked about the letter Hilary had received, the previous Tuesday, from a language school in southern Italy.

'I'd go by train,' Barnie said. 'Or by coach. I might take a coach through France.'

Barnie told Jas by Anne Hathaway's front door. The garden was narrow and stuffed with tall flowers. The others were upstairs wondering how people had ever coped with such low ceilings and uneven floors. There were two bees buzzing in the hollyhocks by the garden path. The gravel coach park next to the cottage swarmed with tourists. In his mind, Barnie lit a fuse and clapped his hands over his ears.

'Why didn't you tell me before?' Jas's voice sounded shaky.

'There was never the opportunity,' Barnie explained.

'There was any evening last week. . .'

'You don't take any notice of me.'

Jas laughed and pulled a weed from between the bricks in the path.

'I'd have listened to you if you'd told me that. Syphilis, for Christ's sake! And you wait till we're in Anne Hathaway's front garden!'

'She won't mind,' Barnie said rashly. 'They were all *born* with it in those days.'

'You deliberately waited until we were with other people so we couldn't discuss it,' Jas said.

'Yeah, that was probably cowardly.'

'Fucking right it was cowardly!'

'But I've told you now.'

Jas looked wild with anger. 'You let me go on without telling me! I should have gone to the clinic straight away. Didn't they tell you that? Didn't they want to know who else was involved?'

'I've told you,' Barnie said. 'It was the French coach driver in London.'

Jas snorted contemptuously. 'Yeah?'

'A month ago.'

'So?'

'So what's happened in the last month?'

'What are you talking about?'

'How many times have we had any kind of sex in the last month?'

Jas looked at him blankly. The bees hummed loudly in the hollyhocks.

'No, you hadn't noticed, had you?' Barnie said. 'We haven't, that's the answer. We haven't had sex once. And you hadn't even noticed.'

A Japanese woman passed them on the path. She didn't touch them but she apologised all the same and smiled broadly. Jas smiled back.

'In fact,' Barnie continued, 'I can't remember when we last *did* have sex.'

Jas looked towards the door, embarrassed.

'And you didn't say anything!' he whispered. 'You didn't tell me, did you?'

'Christ, if you hadn't noticed, what was the point?' Barnie said. 'You don't notice anything. You fill the flat with things you've bought from the latest mail order catalogue; you talk about buying a house; you talk about decorating the hall. *Your* money, *your* house and *your* hall. Nothing belongs to me. I'm twenty-two and I've got nothing of my own. I just drifted along. And you've got used to me, like you've got used to your food blender and your compact disc player. I'm sorry, but I've had enough.'

'What do you mean?'

'I'm sorry, I'm just not interested any more. Not enough to try and put things right. You're always on about me being young and irresponsible. You're not going to make me feel guilty about that.'

Ingeborg called down from one of the upstairs windows, 'Hi! Come on up.'

Jas smiled up at her. 'Maybe in a minute.'

'You look miserable!' she said. 'Come up to the bedroom.'

'Tart!' Barnie said.

'For Christ's sake, what's wrong with you? At least make an effort to do your job.'

'Effort?' Barnie said, incredulously. 'Who are you to talk about effort? If you'd made any effort, we might not be in this situation.'

'So how many have there been apart from the coach driver?'

'None,' Barnie said. 'But I can't take any more of being ignored. What's the point of going on if we're not happy?'

90

'But I thought we were,' Jas said. 'The day I brought the compact disc player home, I thought how pleased you'd be. I bought it for *us*. And the blender, and the other things.'

He knew he shouldn't before he did it, but Barnie threw back his head and laughed out loud till his voice echoed up and down Anne Hathaway's garden path. Charlotte, emerging from the front door, stared blankly at him. Hilary, following close behind, turned to Jas, who was watching the bees circling above the hollyhocks. She took hold of his arm and said, gently:

'You look hot, Jas. I've got a can of Vimto in my bag. D'you want some?'

The Balance of Trade

Andrew Owtram stopped half-way along the concrete path and kicked something onto the frosty grass.

'It's a johnny,' Lewis said.

'Yeah, I can see that.' Andrew watched his breath hanging in the still air. 'Just wondered what it was doing outside the café. . .'

Lewis arched his eyebrows and smiled.

'I've brought birds down 'ere at night-time in the past,' he said, as they made their way towards the café door. 'It's handy after a West End party. Not in this weather, of course – in the summer, more. There's a dark bit round the other side of the café. You 'ave to go somewhere quiet 'cos of the park police. They've got their own park station over there.' He screwed up his eyes and looked across the grass towards a belt of trees. The red outline of a building was just visible where dying leaves had fallen from the branches. 'I remember I brought a bird up 'ere one night last year,' he chuckled. Andrew noticed his right hand sink into the deep pocket of his tweed coat. 'Secretary at the last place I worked at. We 'ad a staff party for one of the directors who was leaving. This girl'd been hot for me for weeks – coming on right strong she was, at the party. I managed to get 'er on one side and asked 'er if she fancied a walk down 'ere afterwards. Fuck me, she was hot for it!' He chuckled again and whistled through his teeth as if he could scarcely believe the memory. 'I 'ad her up against that wall over there, and fuck me if she didn't. . .'

A police patrol van swept along the lakeside path. A balding man in a red tracksuit and white headband jogged past, a portable phone swinging from a belt at his waist. A middle-aged man and woman, both wrapped in fur coats and scarves, passed the two men as they stood on the path. They looked Latin and cold.

'Come on,' Andrew said. 'I need a decent cup of coffee after the muck we had in that hotel.'

A faint touch of October sunshine flickered across the dark water of the Serpentine as they opened the glass door and entered the warmth of the lakeside café.

Synthesised carol tunes were seeping through speakers in the ceiling. Someone had arranged a thin string of purple tinsel around the central cash register. The café smelled of coffee and stale cakes. There were very few customers. The Latin-looking couple were standing by the self-service counter, slowly unbuttoning their coats and peering dubiously through the perspex flaps. A dark-haired girl with huge white hoop ear-rings sat on a stool by the till, turning her head aerobically from side to side. She had her eyes closed. An older woman in a blue overall was wiping trays with a cloth, humming along to the music.

The edge of a metal chair caught against Lewis's briefcase, leaving a long thin gash across the black leather.

'Fuck it! That's the second buggered briefcase this month!'

'Try black boot polish,' Andrew said. 'It'll never show. I'm using the briefcase I used for school.'

Lewis glanced down at the article in question. 'I was gonna mention it,' he said. 'Before Pegrum does. I saw 'im looking at it yesterday at the meeting.'

'Why?' Andrew said. 'What's wrong with it?' They'd reached the beginning of the counter.

'Well, it's a bit antiquated, innit?' Lewis said. 'Needs wheels, that does. Not exactly portable. It's not *streamlined*, you see.' He ran his finger along the tray ridge, and his gold rings flashed under the display lights. 'I fancy a burger.'

The woman watched them from behind the counter and wiped her trays clean. It was nice to see a bit of quality for a change – businessmen, instead of yobbos and thick tourists who could never count their money out properly.

It was only eleven fifteen, but she wouldn't mind betting these two would order the Executive Grill Platter. The flash one with the rings and the tan especially – you could see he had a big appetite. . .

'What's it to be, gentlemen?'

'Just a coffee, please,' Andrew said, 'and a Chelsea bun.'

The woman sighed quietly. 'Nothing hot? Cold morning like this?'

'Watching our waist-lines,' Lewis said.

'You speak for yourself,' Andrew replied.

'Oh well, coffee and a Chelsea.' The woman reached into one of the display cabinets with a pair of tongs and extracted a bun. It bounced slightly as it hit the plate. Then she looked at Lewis. 'And what about you, sir? Can't tempt you to *anything* hot?'

'Not unless the cashier comes on toast.'

The woman didn't even blink. 'Sounds like your friend's heard that line before, by the look on his face,' she said.

Andrew blushed and moved along the counter to where the Latin-looking couple were searching their pockets for change.

'We're doing a seasonal special, if you're interested,' the woman continued. 'Monster Mince Pies. Only thirty-five p. I can whip one through the microwave for you in seconds. Squirt of cream, decorative holly leaf with realistic red berry, and Bob's yer uncle.'

'Hang about,' Lewis said. 'It's still only October.'

'Market forces,' the woman said, matter-of-factly, her face disappearing briefly behind a column of steam from the hot water dispenser. 'We start the kiddies' Christmas parties in a fortnight. Lots of the people over Kensington way are abroad for Christmas, you see. It's a question of fitting it all in. I bet busy executives like you would prefer a staggered Christmas if you were honest – now wouldn't you?'

'Christmas all the time for me, love,' Lewis said.

The woman glanced again at the gold rings on his fingers and said, 'Lucky you.'

There was a row developing at the till. The cashier was peering into a coffee cup; the Latin-looking couple were staring at her with surprised expressions.

'What did you ask for?' the girl said. 'It looks like coffee to me.'

'Two cappuccino,' the man said, in a thick Mediterranean accent.

'One moment.' The girl slid off the stool. ' 'ear that, Reen?'

The older woman looked round from the water dispenser. 'Sorry love, did I mix them up?'

'They wanted cappuccinos.'

'Bring the cups 'ere,' the woman whispered, 'and apologise to the gentleman.'

'I'm sorry,' the girl called to the couple, 'I'm new.' She gave them a sickly smile and took the cups back to Reen. 'So the cappuccino's the one with the brown stuff on top?'

'You just shove some of the scum from the hot milk jug on the top and sprinkle a bit of drinking chocolate on it.'

'What a performance!'

'Well, it's twenty p. extra. . .'

'Really?' The girl looked happier. She took the revised cups of coffee back to the couple. 'That's one sixty, please. It's slightly more pricey because it's foreign.'

Lewis sidled up to the till and winked at the girl.

Andrew sat down at one of the window tables and undid his left shoelace. He could feel a blister forming on the side of his big toe where the leather had cut into his skin. He sat and gazed out of the window at the dark water of the Serpentine, rubbing his toes and wondering how others managed, year after year, in sensible shoes. There were certain things he wouldn't do: he wouldn't wear anything but black socks with his suit and he'd never, ever wear slip-ons. Unlike Lewis. . .

'I'm fucked, I am,' Lewis said, placing two cups of pale brown coffee on the table. He took off his coat and draped it over the back of a vacant chair, positioning it carefully so that the bottom cleared the floor. He unbuttoned his jacket and Andrew noticed the outline of his stomach pressing against his striped shirt. Something made him want to ask Lewis where he had his highlights done, though he wasn't really interested. He decided it was because Lewis would probably resent the question. He left it unsaid.

'Did you take any notes this morning?' Lewis asked, when he'd finally sat down. 'Didn't see you write much.'

'I made a few,' Andrew said, still gazing through the window. 'There wasn't much new, really, was there?'

'Well,' Lewis said, a warning tone to his voice, 'Pegrum's testing us on it tomorrow. 'E told us 'e would. . .'

Andrew looked at him and shrugged. 'I'll be all right.'

'You're a bit of a rebel, really, aren't you, Andy boy? I've noticed. There's something different about you. You're not like the others.'

Andrew bit his lip. 'How d'you mean?'

'Oh, I dunno,' Lewis said. 'Don't get me wrong, I'm not criticising you or anything, but you don't seem too – 'ow do I put it? – *keyed in* to the job. Know what I mean?'

Andrew shrugged his shoulders again. Lewis didn't seem to have noticed him blushing – he was now trying to balance a teaspoon on the rim of the sugar bowl.

'Well, I take it seriously, of course,' Andrew said. He thought he sounded hopelessly unconvincing, but still Lewis didn't seem to have noticed anything. 'I'm as committed as anyone. Perhaps I just don't show it. . .'

Lewis looked up. 'Yeah, that's probably it.'

The chairs and sunshades had been removed from the tables on the terrace, locked up somewhere for the winter. Now the metal tables were streaked with bird shit and dried rain, but Andrew couldn't see any birds this morning. The trees along the far edge of the Serpentine looked like enormous dead twigs. The only things that moved were a styrofoam cup, bobbing gently on the dark water, and a police van sliding across the horizon against the grey sky.

'Getting yer debts paid off, then?' Lewis said.

'Slowly.'

'Never ends, does it? Course, you're better off than some people not running a car. Mind you, beats me 'ow you get all yer visits done, using British Rail.'

'I get by,' Andrew said. 'At least I don't have the hassle of trying to find places to park.'

Lewis nodded. 'That's true. *And* you don't have the expense. Fuck me! That car of mine costs me an arm an' a leg. Don't know why I bother. If I didn't need it for work, I probably wouldn't bother. Not with the new light railway link and that. It's a piece a cake getting into the city from where I live.'

'Yeah, I suppose it is. . .'

'No problem! Mind you, if I got rid of the Porsche, Jill'd go mental. Where's your place?'

'Rotherhithe.'

'That's right. Not too hot on the public transport there, I don't suppose.'

'Oh it's not too bad,' Andrew said. 'The railway line runs right behind the mews.'

Lewis looked impressed. 'That's handy,' he said. ' 'Ow much did you say you'd made on it since you moved in?'

'Thirty thousand,' Andrew said. 'According to the estate agents.'

'There you are, then,' Lewis said. 'You should think about moving on. You could come my way a bit.'

'But I've only been there a year.'

'Never too soon, Andy boy. Property's not the safe bet it was a year ago. . .'

Andrew sighed quietly. 'I'll stick where I am for a bit longer, I think,' he said.

'Well, you know best, mate. Still, bet yer bird doesn't like you being so far away, does she?'

'Oh, she's got a car,' Andrew said, trying to control his voice. 'That's no problem.'

'Lives in at the hospital, does she?'

'No, she shares a flat with two of the other nurses.'

Lewis grinned. 'So there's no problem sneakin' out the nurse's hostel first thing. I've done that a few times before now!'

'Yeah?' Andrew said. He wasn't surprised.

Three young men in faded jeans and old leather jackets appeared at the café door. Reen looked up from her newspaper and scowled. Suddenly the café was noisy.

Two of the men had cameras slung over their shoulders; the third was carrying a maroon portfolio. The smell of Old Holborn wafted across the café. Lewis tutted quietly. Andrew turned his head away from the newcomers and stared through the window, hoping that Lewis hadn't noticed his look of surprise.

'Three coffees, please,' one of the men said, 'and three monstrous mince pies.' One of the others sniggered and blew on his fingers.

'S'pose he thought that was clever,' Lewis murmured. 'Cos of that sign on the counter: *Monster Mince Pies*, see?'

'Yeah,' Andrew said.

The three men paid the girl and sat down a few tables away from Andrew and Lewis. Andrew knew he couldn't look away for ever, so he turned his face towards the newcomers. The one with black greased-back hair and the stubbly chin recognised him immediately and smiled. Andrew managed the smallest, most discreet smile he could in reply and glanced quickly at Lewis. The young man nodded slightly. He understood. Lewis had again noticed nothing.

'You know,' Lewis said, 'we ought to get together one evening – all four of us. I'm sure Jill'd get on with your bird – wha's her name again?'

'Sue.'

'I told you Jill used to be an 'ospital receptionist.'

'Did she?'

'Oh yeah. St Thomas's.'

'Right. . .'

'Well, we'll 'ave to fix something up one night. Dinner and a club – something like that.'

'Sounds good,' Andrew said. 'It's just always a bit difficult knowing when Sue's working. You know what it is with nurses.'

'Fuck me, don't I just! I remember one bird I used to know. Worked in the Royal Free. . .'

The tape of Christmas carols came to an end. Reen put down her paper again and went to turn it back to the beginning. The young man with the greased black hair kept looking at Andrew.

'I reckon so, anyway. What d'you think? 'Ave you noticed anything?'

'Sorry?'

'Pegrum,' Lewis said. 'I reckon 'e's got it in for me. Thinks I'm too much of a rough diamond, I can tell.'

'Oh, I don't think so,' Andrew said.

'There's something 'e doesn't like about me. Just wondered if *you'd* noticed anything.'

'Can't say I have.'

'I reckon 'e wishes 'e was my age again. 'Ow old d' yer think 'e is? Forty-five? I bet 'e looks at me and wishes e'd 'ad what I've got at twenty-six. I mean, I 'aven't done badly, 'ave I? For a Dagenham boy?'

Andrew laughed. What did he want him to say? 'You've done very well.'

'*I* reckon I 'ave. . .' Lewis reached for his coat. 'Can't sit 'ere all day. Onus on the bonus, like Pegrum says. I've got a call to do in Barking, and that's me done for the day. Easy for getting home.'

Andrew watched him button up his coat. 'I'll stay a few minutes,' he said. 'I'm heading towards Ken High Street.'

'You sure?' Lewis said. 'I can give you a lift easy, down to Barker's.'

'No, I'm all right, thanks,' Andrew said. 'Cheers.'

'I'll be off, then. Oh, don't forget when we're in the office tomorra – 'ave a look at Pegrum. I'm *sure* 'e's got it in for me.'

'I'll have a look,' Andrew said.

'Cheers.' Lewis picked up his briefcase and made for the café door. He winked again at the cashier. On his way out, he brushed against the Latin-looking couple's table. ' 'Scuse I'.

The young man with the greased black hair shifted out of his seat and wandered over to Andrew's table. They grinned at one another.

'Surprise, surprise.'

Andrew glanced quickly through the window. Lewis had disappeared.

'You don't mind me coming over, do you?'

99

'No, not at all,' Andrew said. 'It's good to see you again.'
The man smiled. 'So you remember me, then?'

'Of course. It's Patrick, isn't it? I remember you.'

'I didn't come over when your friend was with you. . .'

'He's not a friend,' Andrew said. 'I just work with him. He's definitely not what I'd call a friend.'

'Mind if I sit down?'

'Go ahead.'

Patrick slid into the seat and sat with his elbows on the table, smiling at Andrew. 'I know what you're thinking,' he said. 'You're thinking how scruffy I look. I always make an effort when I see people. . .'

Andrew laughed. 'I'm not thinking that. *You're* probably thinking what a pillock I look dressed in a suit.'

'You look great. Want some coffee?'

'No thanks, I've been drinking it all morning.'

'Me too,' Patrick said, with a quick look back at his friends. 'We've been photographing the exhibition at the Serpentine Gallery.'

'Oh, yeah?'

'I shouldn't bother going if I were you. It's crap.'

'I used to go to galleries,' Andrew said, 'before I got this job. I hardly ever think about art these days.' He frowned. 'I hadn't realised till now. . .'

Patrick shrugged his shoulders. 'Well, you're a busy man, what with one thing and another. So what's the job?'

'A firm of private financial consultants. I went along to one of their recruitment afternoons after I saw their ad in *The Standard*. It said I could earn over twenty K a year and have a flash car.'

Patrick smiled, but he didn't say anything.

'We go round to people's houses and convince them they're heading for ruin if they don't take financial advice from us. To keep them with us, we send them birthday cards and anniversary cards and phone them up when there's a birth or a death in the family. We have huge files on every client.'

'That sounds sinister. . .'

'It's revolting,' Andrew said. 'This morning Lewis and I

were at a hotel near Hyde Park Corner listening to some American wanker talking about the very latest in one-to-one communication tactics.'

Patrick played with the sugar bowl. 'Doesn't sound like you're very fond of the job. . .' he said.

Andrew laughed. 'And you're probably wondering why I do it.'

'Sort of. . .'

'Well, like I told you when we met, I've got a mortgage and a lot of credit to pay off.'

'Funny,' Patrick said. 'You didn't strike me as being that type of person.'

Andrew laughed again. 'What type of person?'

'I don't know,' Patrick said. 'I'm just surprised you're one of the people stuck with a mortgage and huge bills hanging round your neck.'

'See, it can happen to the best of us,' Andrew said. 'I was surprised to find myself in that state too.'

'But how did it happen?' Patrick asked. 'I see all the *Panorama* programmes about house repossession and credit card defaulters and I wonder how people manage to get themselves in that condition.' He noticed Andrew's expression and added: 'I'm sorry. This isn't any of my business, is it?'

'Oh, it's all right,' Andrew said, looking glum. 'I wonder, too. Weak-willed, I suppose. All the people I went to college with have got homes and good jobs and I just let myself be persuaded that I needed them too. I got frightened not having any real possessions. It's pathetic, isn't it?'

Patrick shrugged his shoulders again. 'We all need *some* possessions,' he said. 'I mean, you saw my place when you came round that time. Full of shit I've accumulated over years.'

'I liked your flat. . .' Andrew said; and Patrick grinned.

Two nuns hurried past the café; rubbing their hands. The Latin-looking couple got up and left.

'The trouble is,' Andrew said, 'I have to tell so many lies. That bloke Lewis who was here just now, he's a real wanker.'

'He looked it,' Patrick said, gravely.

'I have to pretend I'm straight and have a girlfriend and everything. All he talks about is screwing birds in the back of his Porsche. I feel ashamed of myself when I think about the lies I tell, but there's no way they'd have me if they knew the truth. They're a terrible company to work for. Even Lewis reckons they're out to get him. . .'

'Why?'

'Oh, 'cos he's a working-class boy made good and he reckons the directors think he's flash and pushy.'

'I thought the whole point of the job was to be pushy,' Patrick said.

'It is,' Andrew said, 'but you've got to do it subtly. You saw what Lewis was like.'

'Ever thought of doing some sort of work like mine?' Patrick asked.

Andrew laughed. 'You're joking, aren't you? I don't think it's really me, somehow.'

Patrick shrugged his shoulders.

'I'll have to go now,' Andrew said. 'I'm making for Ken High Street. It's a bit of a walk.'

'Mind if I walk with you? I can catch a bus home at the Albert Hall.'

'Why not?'

Patrick picked up his camera and said goodbye to his friends. Andrew noticed one of them raise an eyebrow and smile. He kept his eyes firmly on the door as they left the café. Reen watched them leave from behind the counter. Now, that really *was* strange. . .

The air was still cold outside. There was no sun on the water now. Andrew buttoned up his coat and Patrick zipped up his battered leather jacket. He pulled a long red scarf from his bag and wound it round his neck. They joined the path and walked briskly in the direction of the bridge.

'You were a sight better than most I see,' Patrick said.

Andrew smirked. 'Do you see many, then?'

'Not so many these days. I'm getting too busy with all this.' He patted his camera.

'Well, I enjoyed it too,' Andrew said. 'So. . .'

'Yeah?'

'Yeah.'

'Tonight any good?' Patrick said.

'Tonight would be fine. Say about eight?'

'All right.'

'There's one thing I wanted to ask. . .' Andrew said.

'Yeah?'

'Well, I just wonder why you *do* it. I mean, I know it's none of my business, or anything. . .'

Patrick shrugged his shoulders and laughed. 'I sometimes wonder that,' he said. 'I've been doing it off and on for about ten years. It just turns me on, I suppose. The idea of the money changing hands. . . I don't know. . .'

They walked in silence for a few moments. Another man jogged past in the opposite direction. He was panting heavily and looked angry.

'My place or yours?' Andrew said.

'I'll come to yours if you like,' Patrick said. 'We'll stop on the bridge and you can give me your address.'

'You know,' Andrew said, 'I decided this morning – when we were at the training session – I'm leaving the company. I'm not going in to head office tomorrow – never again. I'm throwing it in. It's too much of a strain pretending – trying to keep up with people like Lewis.'

'Congratulations,' Patrick said. 'What will you do for money?'

Andrew smiled at him. 'Go full-time, I suppose.'

'You'll be putting your rates up, then?'

'Oh *you'll* be all right,' Andrew said. 'I'll think of you as a regular.'

'Easy,' Patrick said. 'I get bored quickly. It's only fair you know that.' Then he laughed. 'But I'm not bored yet.'

Lewis hurried a little further along the narrow path to where it disappeared into a thicket of trees. He put his briefcase down on a bench and buttoned his coat to the neck against the cold, still air. The leaves on the trees were mustard yellow; they scraped against his skin as he parted the lower twigs and peered through the gap towards the main path. Andrew and the scruffy man were strolling towards the bridge. Andrew had slung his briefcase over one shoulder, like a schoolboy. They looked at one another and talked a lot. He watched them until they disappeared under the bridge, and then he sat down on the bench.

He undid his briefcase and pulled out a cordless telephone. He looked around to make sure he was alone and then keyed in the number.

'Mr Pegrum, please. . . Oh, I think 'e'll be available to talk to me. Tell 'im it's Lewis Turner.' There was a pause. Lewis looked at the gash on the briefcase.

'Mr Pegrum? Lewis Turner 'ere. . . Yeah, yeah it went very well. Very useful, I thought. . . I'll be off to Barking in a while. I believe it's Mrs Unwin's birthday today, so I'm takin' 'er a card with the compliments of the company. I just thought you'd like to know I've done what you asked. . . You were right about 'im. . . I didn't get anything out of him *verbally*, but 'e's definitely not *us*. . . Definitely not. It's his attitude and everything. I can't put me finger on it, but there's *something* wrong. I think you're right to get rid of 'im. I'm with you all the way. . . And another thing. We've just 'ad coffee in the place by the Serpentine. There was a right bunch of scruffy characters in there – real layabouts. Anyway, I left to come and phone you, and I just saw Owtram leave the café with one of these jokers. Walked off together – in the *same* direction. . . Well, I wouldn't like to 'azard a guess on that one, Mr Pegrum. Mind you, they looked just like trouble-makers to me – left-wingers, probably. You know the type. . . Well, that's what I'm wondering. . . Well, all right. . . Not at all, Mr Pegrum. Seems you were quite right to be suspicious. It showed real insight, that did. . . There was just *one* other thing. 'Bout this evening. . . Tha's right. Where are you talking from? . . . The toilet? All right. Still on, then, is it? . . . 's right. My place at eight.'

Lewis looked round quickly again and leaned back on the bench, smiling. 'Now listen carefully. I'll be waiting for you in those army fatigues – so don't be late, you arse-lickin' bastard. Understand?'

Safe as Houses

They noticed one another at the same time. Brian was leaning in his usual place beside the fruit machine. He was drinking from a bottle of American lager, left hand stuck in the pocket of his Levis. He was watching a tattooed skinhead move round the pool table. It was Friday night and he was winding down from a long week at the auction rooms.

The pool match had just come to an end with the skinhead aloof and superior in victory. Brian watched him to see if he'd go down to the dark basement bar – he seemed to be hovering indecisively at the top of the stairs. Brian felt his right leg flex in anticipation. The skin glanced lazily round the bar, giving each face a blank, cursory glance, and then disappeared down the stairs. Brian pushed himself forward from the wall and moved off towards the staircase. He collided with Donald at the far end of the pool table. They stood almost face-to-face, though Donald was several inches taller than Brian.

Donald looked young – no more than twenty-two or three. His face was handsome and empty. Even when he smiled and apologised, there was something vacant about his expression. Brian was used to the non-committal attitudes of most of the people in the bar. It was accepted behaviour – show any kind of openness and it gave too much away. Brian had been around long enough to know the rules. He never questioned them. He smiled back and apologised.

'Sorry,' he said. 'I've made you spill your drink.' There was a wet mark on the boy's white t-shirt.

'So there is.' He seemed surprised for a moment. Then he shrugged his shoulders and gave another thin smile. 'Don't worry.' He held up his glass. 'Look, there isn't much gone.'

Brian meant to move on then, but he didn't. They stood very close and looked at each other.

'Busy tonight,' Brian said.

The boy looked round, as if noticing the other people for the first time. 'Isn't it usually this busy, then?'

'Not until later. When the eleven o'clock pubs close.'

The boy nodded slowly. 'I'm Donald,' he said.

Brian smiled. It was a bit early in the evening for this, but it would help pass the time before the place started to get crowded. Besides, he'd seen the skinhead there lots of times and he never left before closing time. He'd wait. 'Brian.'

'Hi, Brian.'

'Hi.'

'Would you like a drink?' Donald asked.

Well, his bottle was empty. 'OK. I'm on Bud. But I should buy you one, after knocking into you.'

Donald shrugged again. 'Later, maybe.' He ambled off towards the bar, and Brian leaned against the wall at the top of the stairs. Familiar faces passed him and smiled conspiratorially on their way downstairs. The smell of poppers floated up from the cellar. He could feel the thud of disco music vibrating through the walls. He wiped the sweat from his forehead and rubbed his hand over the leg of his jeans. The material felt stiff and clean. Brian had washed all his denim that week and ironed it in one go during *News at Ten* the previous evening. He liked the feel of clean jeans tight against his skin: you never had time to think about your body at work.

Brian hadn't lost his sense of adventure. He was ready when the weekends came around. Of course, it wasn't quite the same these days, but the basic urges hadn't changed. You could still go downstairs and find something in the dark: and if you met someone really special – once a fortnight or so – and the weather was good, you could go off somewhere and enjoy the open air. Brian prided himself on his imagination. It was difficult, sometimes, to believe that the years hadn't dulled his appetite, or that after hundreds of men, he still wanted more.

Another acquaintance passed and smiled. They were all old-timers. Downstairs, you could still do what you wanted if you met the right person. Everyone who went down understood. No one wanted to be the first to spoil the fun: no one wanted to be the first to urge caution. Everyone knew the rules, and you followed them, though if neither of you said anything, you could bend them, just a little. . .

Brian watched Donald return from the bar. He had a good body under those clothes. There was nothing wrong in settling for the first thing that came along – after all, it wasn't as if he were *desperate*. They'd have a drink upstairs and then maybe go down to the cellar. They might even find the skinhead waiting in one of the dark corners. Later, if the rain held off, they could drive to the park, all three of them. . .

Donald had other ideas. Brian found himself sitting down, for the first time, at the chairs by the bar. Another acquaintance walked past, looked at him with vague surprise, and winked.

'I've only been here a couple of times,' Donald said.

'I've never seen you here before. Where do you normally drink?'

'I don't go out to bars much.'

'What do you do instead?'

'Oh, I keep busy, you know. I'm a qualified masseur. The real thing, you know.'

'Really?'

'Yeah. I'm a professional.'

Brian reached into his jacket pocket for his cigarettes. 'So you're having an evening off, are you?'

'Yeah.'

'Do you get much work?'

'Yeah, I'm very busy, but I don't see it as work. It really interests me. It's a science, really.'

'Do you smoke?'

'No, I don't.' The smile faded briefly from Donald's face.

107

'You don't mind if I. . . ?'

Donald shrugged. 'It's up to you. . .'

Brian lit up, all the same.

'And of course,' Donald went on, 'it's safe, isn't it? It's getting much more popular these days. If it's done properly, it's very sexual, even without wanking.'

'So you haven't been downstairs?' Brian said, tentatively.

Donald almost choked on his drink. 'You're joking, aren't you?' he said. There was a pause. 'What do *you* do for a living?'

'I work at one of the auction houses,' Brian said. He didn't feel like talking about it.

'That must be interesting,' Donald said. 'So what exactly do you *do*?'

It wouldn't be the usual kind of Friday evening now, whatever happened. Brian wished he could stand up and walk away, but he was too polite, and part of him was enjoying this novelty. There was something about the blandly handsome young man that wouldn't let him go. Besides, there was always Saturday night.

'Have you always lived in London?' Donald asked him.

'Fifteen years,' Brian said. 'But I grew up in Berkshire.'

'So you must have lots of friends?'

'Oh yes, I know lots of people.'

'I don't,' Donald said. 'I'm usually on my own. I don't meet many people I feel I can really get on with. Do you know what I mean?'

'Yes. . .'

'After all, most people are trash, aren't they?'

Brian stared at him. He wondered if he'd heard the boy correctly.

'I mean, when it comes down to it, most people aren't *worth* getting to know.'

'That sounds a bit cynical,' Brian said, trying to sound amused.

'Don't we have reason to be cynical?' Donald asked. He looked very serious.

'I wasn't like that at your age. How old *are* you? Twenty-two?'

'Twenty-one,' Donald said. 'All *this* was waiting for

you at twenty-one – a big adventure to your generation. The possibility of it all going wrong never entered your heads.'

'Well, it's not easy for any of us, these days,' Brian said. Donald looked towards the cellar stairs and then back at Brian, but he said nothing.

'We're all in the same boat. . .'

'But you've had years of freedom, haven't you?' Above the sound of the thudding disco music, Brian detected a note of accusation in the boy's voice. He felt irritated for a moment, but then Donald's expression changed.

'That's why I'm into massage,' he said, smiling. 'It's a challenge. I don't see it as making the best of things, like some people do. *They* don't have the technique of the commitment. Like I say, they're not worth getting to know. But you're different, Brian. I mean, look at us sitting here chatting away. I'm not interested in people I can't *talk* to.'

'Can I get you that drink now?'

'You could invite me back to your place. . .'

Brian laughed nervously. 'But it's only just gone midnight. . .' he said, knowing it sounded feeble.

'I'm sorry,' Donald said, glancing back at the top of the stairs again. 'You might have other things to do. I didn't think. I'm sorry. . .' He started to get up.

'No,' Brian said, quickly, 'it's not that. I'm just used to staying here late.'

Donald smiled. 'So, are you going to invite me back? I could show you what I know about massage.'

'Yeah . . . yeah, why not?'

They pulled up in a street of small Georgian houses near Maida Vale and Donald said: 'This looks nice. You've got yourself well established.'

'Well, I should have by now,' Brian said, unclipping his seat-belt.

'It's a nice area, this,' the boy continued. 'I massaged a politician near here once.'

'Did you?'

'I'm sorry, but I can't say who it was. His shoulders were

in a chronic state. You keep a light on when you're out, then?' They were standing on the pavement, at the foot of a flight of stone steps.

'Yes. . .'

'Yeah, it's a nice place.' Donald nodded approvingly. 'You're a home lover, aren't you?'

'I suppose I am,' Brian said, slipping the key into the front-door lock.

'I thought so,' Donald said. 'You're not scared of your own company, like lots of people are.'

'I don't often have people back,' Brian said, as they entered the hall.

'I'm honoured.'

Warm air rushed past Brian's face as he closed the door. It was barely two hours since he'd gone out; almost six months since he'd brought someone home. He didn't quite know how this had happened.

The two living rooms had been knocked into one and papered in Regency stripe. The marble fireplace in the front was original, but the back one was a modern copy. Donald was urged to inspect them carefully and compare. No, he admitted, you'd never be able to tell.

'It cost a fortune,' Brian said, 'but I found a gay stone-mason who needed the work, so it was worth it on all sides. It made the room look . . . *balanced* and helped the pink economy at the same time.'

Donald sat down. 'Yes,' he said, 'I like balance. This is nice.' He ran his hand over the silk fabric of the sofa.

'It's quite unusual,' Brian said. He took off his leather jacket and folded it neatly on the sofa. 'I was shopping in Kingston one Saturday and came across this marvellous upholsterer.'

'Is it silk?'

'Sort of silk. I can't remember, exactly. . .'

'And what colour would you say it is, Brian? It's sort of electric blue, isn't it?'

'Well, more *petrol* I'd call it. Are you interested in interior design, then?'

Donald looked at him with a bland smile. 'No,' he said.

110

Brian suddenly felt a bit dizzy. 'Do you want a cold drink? I'm sweating. There's no air tonight. . .'

'Do you have any fruit juice?'

'Orange, grapefruit, Tropical Mix or English Country Apple?' Brian counted them out on his fingers.

'Apple, I think.' Donald had kicked off his shoes and settled down into the sofa.

'Right . . . won't be a moment. Make yourself at home.'

'Cheers, Brian.'

On the way upstairs, Donald asked Brian if he had any candles. 'They're great for atmosphere,' he explained.

They stopped by a cupboard on the landing, and Brian produced a box of candles.

'I bought them for the candlelight AIDS vigil,' he said, turning the box over in his hand.

'It's a new box. . .'

'I couldn't make it . . . at the last moment.'

'It was very moving.'

Brian's bedroom was at the back of the house. The carpet and the duvet cover on the futon were powder blue, and the curtains were the same as the fabric on the sofa downstairs.

'What did we do before dimmer switches?' Brian said, reducing the light to a soft yellow glow. Donald noticed how much younger Brian looked in the dark.

The room smelt of aftershave and stale cigarette smoke. On the low table beside the futon was a white saucer caked in ash, a digital alarm clock, a Jeffrey Archer novel, a collection of cologne bottles and a second saucer, full of pound coins.

One of the fireplace recesses contained a set of open box-compartments. Each one had a special function: one compartment held pullovers, all carefully folded; another was full of socks rolled into neat balls; a third was devoted to leather thongs, metal cock rings and a jumble of silver chains. The other recess served as an open wardrobe. On the left of the clothes rail were a number of suits. After these came white shirts, coloured shirts, t-shirts, casual jackets, denim shirts and jackets, jeans, leather

111

waistcoats, and finally two more leather jackets. The row of shoes on the floor reflected the clothes above, starting with smart black work shoes and ending with a pair of black rubber waders.

Donald looked round the room and nodded thoughtfully. 'You're very organised and methodical, aren't you? I like that. *I'm* a very methodical person. . .'

'You have to be,' Brian explained, 'when you live in such a small place. Where do you live?'

'I have a bedsit – in Cricklewood.'

'I don't think I've ever been to Cricklewood.'

'It's a spiritual desert,' Donald said, lifting a dumbbell from the floor. 'And the shopping's lousy. No haberdashers *there*. So you work out?' He performed two very controlled bicep curls and then held the dumbbell in his hand for a moment, as if considering the weight, before replacing it on the floor.

'Not as often as I should,' Brian said. 'I always mean to join a gym – a friend of mine goes to one three times a week, and he's always telling me I should go along with him, but. . .'

'Somehow there's never the time, is there?' Donald smiled at him. 'It's the same old story. Always something else to do.'

Brian laughed: 'That's it.' He couldn't tell if Donald was sympathising or criticising.

'Can we use this saucer for a couple of candles?'

'Yeah. Shall I go down and get another?'

'No,' Donald said. 'A couple in here will be fine.' He looked at Brian and smiled. 'Are you all right, Brian? You look very serious.'

'Yes, I'm fine,' Brian said. 'You're just a bit . . . different from most people I've met.'

Donald smiled and lit a candle. 'Don't tell me you're nervous – an experienced man like you?'

'No, of course not,' Brian said, laughing quickly. 'You're just a change from most guys.'

'The thing is, Brian – like I said before – I'm a new generation, aren't I? Post-AIDS: more honest, open, responsible. Because we've all got to be.' He stuck two candles onto the saucer with melted wax. 'People of my age have to forget the things we've missed out on – the things *you've* enjoyed.'

'In some ways,' Brian said, tentatively, 'it makes it easier for you if you've never known things any other way.'

Donald looked round and stared at him. 'But it's still there, isn't it?' he said. 'Look at this evening. Those guys going down to the cellar bar. We all know what still goes on in dark corners and toilets.'

It was a unique sensation for Brian to feel uncomfortable in his own home. 'I know,' he said. 'But there were as many people of your age going down as . . . well . . . of mine. . .' He waited for Donald's reaction. The boy nodded, but his expression remained unchanged.

'Well, that's true,' he said. 'Before I met you, I *did* go down and took a look. Some guys tried to get me to join in. . .'

'. . . can't say I blame them,' Brian said, regretting it at once.

'. . . and I felt angry. That's the word, Brian – *angry*. It was like they wanted my approval.' He placed the saucer, with its two burning candles, beside the futon. 'They didn't get it. Why don't you switch off the light?'

Donald went out to the bathroom and Brian sat down on the bed to unlace his boots. He'd repeated the procedure countless times over the years – coming home from a bar alone or with someone else, and sitting down to begin the slow process of removing his DMs. He'd never felt uncomfortable in his leather gear before, but this evening he couldn't wait to get it off. The boots felt heavy and the waistcoat stiff, like thick cardboard. He put them in a corner of the room and lay back on the mattress, watching the flickering shadows from the candles lick across the ceiling.

Donald was naked. He closed the door quietly and placed his bundle of clothes on the chair by the window. Then he moved, smiling, across to the bed.

'You've got a great body,' Brian said, looking him up and down. 'Like a swimmer.'

'Thanks,' Donald said, matter-of-factly. 'I look after myself.' He held out a bottle of baby oil. 'I found this in the bathroom. Can I use it to massage you?'

'Yeah,' Brian said. 'Only let me get a towel to put on the bed.'

Donald moved back to the chair. 'I brought one with me,' he said. 'I thought you might want to put a towel down.' Brian watched the boy's cock swing gently from side to side as he walked. It didn't arouse him as he might have expected; but there was *something* exciting. . .

Donald spread the towel across the duvet.

'Why don't you take off your clothes? Lie down and I'll massage your back. I noticed the tension in your neck at the bar.'

'Did you?'

'None of us moves properly. We shouldn't be standing, after all. We're animals, really: that's what we're struggling against.'

'I suppose so. . .'

'Take off your clothes.'

The towel was soft and still warm from being in the airing cupboard. It smelt of fabric conditioner. Brian kept his eyes open for the first few minutes. In the candle-light he could just make out the rough weave of the towel and the smooth, almost shiny surface of the duvet cover. Donald was behind him: he could feel the boy straddling his legs and reaching across to the table for the oil bottle. It was too late, now, to run down to the kitchen and get the poppers from his jacket pocket. Besides, Donald would probably feel insulted if he suggested it.

'Now, just relax. When was the last time you had a massage?'

'I can't remember. . . A while ago, now. . .'

'You'll never've had one like this.'

Something cold trickled down his spine.

'You're not in bad shape.'

Brian heard himself snigger awkwardly into the towel.

114

'Cheers.' He became aware of vague, needle-like sensations up and down his back, and he held his breath.

'Relax. . .'

They were Donald's fingers, gliding across his oiled skin, tracing the line of his backbone, gently up and down. He closed his eyes. There were hands now – whole palms sweeping in slow circles up towards his neck. He smelled baby oil and the candle burning on the table beside him.

'Feel good?'

'Hmm. . .'

'See? You're relaxing already.'

'Hmm. . .'

'Like to do this for me some time?'

'Yeah. . .'

'Yeah. Maybe you will.'

It was very quiet. Brian listened to his breath hitting the folds of the towel, and the soft, wet sound of Donald's hands gliding across his skin. From the bedroom next door came the distant sound of time pips on a radio.

'What is it?' he said. 'Two o'clock?'

He heard Donald sigh softly. 'It's one.'

One o'clock. He never usually left the bar before two at the earliest. He thought back over the evening: it hadn't *seemed* any different at the start.

'But what does it matter what time it is?' The hands were working his shoulders now, pressing and pulling until the muscles tingled and relaxed. 'Just forget about what time it is and where you are.'

'Hmm. . . But I was just thinking about my usual Friday nights – going to the bar and. . .' He mumbled into the towel but Donald had heard.

'You don't want to think about the bar, Brian. What can the bar give you? This'll be more exciting than anything you ever found at the bottom of *those* stairs.'

'Yeah?'

'Yeah.'

Brian felt the boy's weight shift. The hands left his neck and moved to the base of his spine. They began circling again, tracing the top curves of his buttocks, squeezing

115

the soft folds of skin, tickling – almost without touching – down between the top of his legs.

'Hmm. . .'

'Yeah, I'll give you real excitement. You never found it, did you? Not really.'

'Sometimes I did,' Brian murmured. 'Sometimes it was. . .'

'But you always knew what you'd find, didn't you? You knew there'd be the same old faces, the same pointless activities. You never really found *satisfaction*, did you? There was no real *danger* – 'cos that's what you were after. A bit of danger.' He was almost whispering. 'And now there's a danger we can't turn on and off when we like. . .'

In his mind, Brian saw the staircase at the bar, with its pitted red carpet and the wall lights where the smoke hung like thick grey cobwebs. For a moment, he was walking down those stairs, brushing against dark bodies on either side; and his heartbeat quickened the further he went down, as it always did. Then a voice was telling him to imagine a new staircase.

'. . . It's a big old house – or a castle. You're standing at the top of the stairs. The walls are built of stone and so are the steps, and down on the left a small window's letting in some light. Can you see that?'

'Yes. . .'

'Can you?'

'Yes, I can.'

'Further down from the window, the stairs turn to the right. It's almost dark down there. You can see where the stairs turn, but you can't see anything else.'

'Hmm. . .'

The hands were sweeping across his body again, up to his neck and back down between his legs, up and down in a steady rhythm.

'You put one foot forward and go down one step. Then another, very slowly. The steps feel hard. Can you smell the air? It's old and musty. You can almost feel yourself cutting through it as you move.'

116

'Hmm. . .'

'You take the steps very slowly and very quietly. You don't make any noise.'

The fingers were trickling round his ears now, running across his temples, flickering softly. The voice sounded far off, somewhere behind him – somewhere back at the top of the stairs.

'You're near the window now. It's a bit lighter, but you still can't see much – just the turn in the stairs, down there. You're still going down, aren't you?'

'Yes.'

'You reach the window, but you don't look out. There's nothing for you outside. You just want to get down those stairs as quietly as you can. . .'

'. . . Down the stairs. . .'

'Slowly, one step at a time.'

He felt cooler now. The air on the stairs was old and damp and smelled of stone. He could sense something moving behind him, and a far-away voice saying 'Slowly . . . one at a time. . .'. Just one hand, now, sweeping in circular movements along his inner thigh.

'Don't stop. Slowly down. You're almost at the turn in the stairs now, aren't you?'

'Hmm. . .'

'The window's behind you. The light's fading. You put your foot forward, and it's the first turning step. You take another. You're in darkness now. Go down another. The window's gone – back round the corner. You wonder what's ahead in the darkness, don't you?'

'Hmm. . .'

'You feel good. You feel excited. Put your foot out, but don't go down.'

'No. . .'

'Feel the excitement. . .'

The towel soaked up Brian's urine like a sponge.

'You're ready to go forward. You. . .'

Something moved behind him again.

'You move forward into the darkness. You don't know there's a big hole in front of you. You're falling. . .'

When Donald brought the edge of the dumbbell down on the back of Brian's neck, there was a funny sound, like the snap of a stud on a leather cock-strap. He stood at the end of the futon for a few moments, watching the man for signs of movement. There were none. He closed his eyes and breathed deeply three times; then he got dressed. Before he left the room, he picked up the Jeffrey Archer novel and stuffed it into his jacket pocket. It was one he hadn't read. He went downstairs. The hall smelled of antiques and furniture polish. The carpet was very soft underfoot.

A fine rain had started to fall. He could hear the ticking of a taxi engine fading in the distance, but the street was deserted. Donald closed the front door quietly behind him, took another deep breath and walked down the seven stone steps to the pavement.

Four More Years

The two men paused when they reached the crest of the hill, and stopped on the rough path beside a field of green corn. They looked back, past the river and the park, to the town.

'You won't find a better view of the old place than that,' the elder of the two said, sticking a thumb into the belt-hook of his dusty jeans. Beyond the shallow valley, where a red and green climbing frame and a see-saw mingled with fragments of ancient abbey wall, the glass in the cathedral windows sparkled like clear water.

A five-minute walk had taken them from the ornamental fishpond by the park gates to what was almost country. Until recently, the other side of the hill had dipped towards unbroken farmland. Now, rows of white-bricked houses punctured the sky like teeth; and towards the south-west, a silver silage factory had destroyed the gentle curve of the horizon.

They could hear the distant hum of traffic in the narrow streets of the medieval town. The sound of a voice, artificially amplified, boomed across the park and then dropped away with the breeze.

'You hear that?' the older man said, wiping sweat from his forehead with the back of his hand. His greying hair looked dusty in the bright light. Adrian knew, without touching it, that it would feel wiry.

Mick was a builder. He was working out in the country, converting three farm-workers' cottages into a weekend home for a London stockbroker. Adrian watched him run his hand over his chest. His skin looked tanned and tight.

He wasn't anything like the other bloke, the sales rep in the light blue Vauxhall, with his puffy, pale skin and the flash stereo with built-in graphic equaliser. It had been pouring with rain that day. The ruts of the farm track had streamed with filthy water and the windows had slowly steamed to the sound of Dire Straits. Now it was June – blazing hot – and Mick was very different.

'You hear that?' Mick said again, cocking his head sideways as the booming voice rippled across the valley. 'They're at it again. They were swarming round the market at dinner-time. I was canvassed three times in the market. One from each party – fair enough, I suppose. . .'

'I saw the Labour candidate by the museum,' Adrian said.

'Did you? I saw her picture in the paper. She looked all right.'

'She was wearing a red dress,' Adrian said. 'She looked depressed.'

'Well, she would here, wouldn't she?' Mick observed. 'I suppose you're not old enough to vote, are you?'

'No,' Adrian said. 'If they'd had the election next year. . .'

'I don't suppose you mind, though, do you?'

'Yes, I do. I want my say as well.'

Mick laughed. 'I know.' He turned to face the boy. 'Well?'

'Where?' Adrian said, looking around.

It was easy to see anyone who might appear on the path from the direction of the park, but behind them it passed through an ancient archway – a solitary fragment of the old abbey, sprouting crazily from the edge of the cornfield – and then turned left, disappearing behind a wall. Anyone could approach from that direction and surprise them.

'It just seems a bit open here.'

There was also the time to think about. He'd promised to meet his mother up in town at five o'clock. Already it was nearly four. Was it really worth the fuss?

120

Mick looked quickly up and down the path, and then at Adrian.

'The corn's quite tall,' he said. 'We could go in the middle of the field.'

'Someone would see us,' Adrian said, dismissively. The idea was exciting all right, but ridiculous. If only they'd been out in the real country. . .

'I like it outside,' Mick said. 'Don't you?'

'Yeah.' Adrian had never done anything outside, except with Denise Blanchard after the village hall disco – and that had been in his parents' carport by the back door, so it hardly counted.

'Where else can we go? Can we meet again – after today?' He hadn't meant to ask. 'We could work out something better.' Mick frowned for a moment; then he broke into a smile.

'Yeah, of course,' he said. 'I'll give you my number later. But what about now?'

The sun had begun to slip towards the distant rooftops of the town, but still it burned hot against their faces. Adrian began to feel uncomfortable.

'We ought to find some shade, wherever we go,' he said. 'It's too hot to stand here.'

'See over there?' Mick said, pointing beyond the park, where a line of trees bordered the river. 'There's one of those wartime shelters by the water. We could go there.'

'That's not really outside, though,' Adrian said.

An elderly woman emerged from the archway, a fox terrier trotting along beside her. She approached them on the path, and Adrian felt suddenly very awkward. It must be obvious, he thought, why they were standing there. Even to an old lady, it must be obvious.

'Good afternoon,' the woman said, brightly. She smiled at them as she passed.

'Afternoon,' Mick replied, giving her a cordial nod. The dog snuffled round his feet and snuffled the leg of his jeans.

'Come on!' the woman called. She walked on, and the

dog scampered obediently after her, its studded collar flashing in the sunshine.

'All right,' Adrian said. 'Let's go there.' He watched the woman descend the hill towards the park. 'Wait till she's a bit further on, eh?'

A sudden gust of wind carried the sound of amplified music from the town centre; then a booming voice, like a banging drum; then more music. The cathedral clock struck four.

The concrete shelter was dark and damp. It felt chilly after the warm sunshine. In contrast to the fresh air outside, it smelt vaguely of mould and urine. After a few minutes, their eyes became accustomed to the dimness. They could make out numerous messages and drawings scribbled on the bare brick walls – mainly crude diagrams of copulating couples, but a few lovingly executed studies of erotic expression. The floor was littered with ice-cream wrappers and contraceptive packets. Through the small slit windows, Adrian saw the branches of a tree quivering slightly in the breeze.

This wasn't what either of them had wanted; and still the ghostly voice was booming across the fields from the town centre. It made Adrian feel as if they were being watched, even here. Well, they could afford to ignore it for a while. Without a word, they stood in the look-out shelter and watched each other undress in the narrow columns of light.

They sat together by the river for a few minutes – a little away from the look-out shelter in case any passer-by guessed what they had done and reported them to the police or to the park-keeper.

Mick told Adrian he was beautiful, and Adrian laughed, embarrassed, because it seemed a funny thing for one bloke to say to another. For a moment, he couldn't look Mick in the face. He threw a twig in the river and watched it float away on the water, until it became caught in a tangle of driftwood and weeds and disappeared.

He asked if they could meet again.

'It doesn't matter about my age, does it?'

'Not to me,' Mick said. 'It doesn't mean anything. Well. . .' He nodded in the direction of the town centre where three noisy campaigns were in progress '. . . only to that lot.'

'That's what some people go for,' Adrian said.

A group of Friesian cows plodded solemnly past on the opposite bank, swishing their tails in rhythm, heading for a clump of shady trees.

Mick laughed. 'It doesn't make any difference to me,' he said. 'You're old enough to know what you're doing, and that makes us equal. I didn't think of your age – I just saw you and knew what I wanted.'

But it was just chance, Adrian thought, that he'd gone to sit by the fishpond. It could just as easily have been someone else.

'Listen, we'll have a return match in four years' time, eh?' Mick said. 'But it won't be any better.'

'Before then,' Adrian said, trying to sound casual.

'Much sooner,' Mick said, lying back on the grass. 'I'll give you my number before we go.'

'I don't know many blokes,' Adrian said. 'There aren't many around here.'

'Not many like you. . .'

'I'm frightened of doing much.'

'I know.'

'It used to be different, didn't it? Easier?'

Mick laughed, and sat up.

'It was different, all right,' he said. 'But I don't know about easier – not in a place like this.'

'But you could do more.'

'Yes, you could,' Mick said. 'But I'm not complaining.' He glanced back at the look-out shelter.

'Oh I'm not *complaining*,' Adrian said quickly, afraid he'd been misunderstood.

'Are you going to stay around here?' Mick asked.

Adrian shrugged his shoulders.

'I might,' he said, and gazed at the river. All his plans to get away had floated off like the twig he'd thrown into the water.

Mick searched in his shirt pocket and brought out a scrap of paper and a biro. He wrote down his number and handed it to Adrian.

'Don't lose it,' he said. 'Give me a call at the weekend, and maybe we could meet up next week. I'll meet you in town if you like, and we can drive out to my place. You can stay if you like. Choose a day when you're not busy.'

'I'm never busy,' Adrian said, cramming the paper into his back pocket. 'It's twenty to five, I'll have to go.'

His mother was waiting, as they'd arranged, by the museum steps. She was sitting on a bench reading the local paper. Under the bench, in the shade, were three plastic carrier bags full of shopping.

'Seen this?' she said, holding the paper out as he sat down beside her. 'Eighteen per cent ahead in a local poll. If I see one more opinion poll, I think I'll scream.'

'It'll be over in a week,' Adrian said.

'They could put a stuffed parrot up in this town, and he'd be eighteen per cent ahead.'

'I thought they had. That's him over there – by the chemist.'

They looked across to the other side of the market, beyond the vegetable stalls and the ice-cream seller by the fountain, to where a group of red-faced shoppers were listening to a man on a platform. He was talking about the Common Agricultural Policy and looking very uncomfortable in his suit and tie. Behind him, two supporters held up a large banner proclaiming 'Four More Years' in large blue letters.

At one of the stalls, a woman attacked the leaves of a cauliflower with a sharp knife. She caught their attention and tutted loudly.

'Four more years, eh?' she called out. 'I wonder where we'll all be in four years' time. I can't see it getting any better, can you?'

'I can't,' Adrian's mother called back. 'Come on – let's get home.'

Adrian picked up two of the bags, and his mother carried the third.

'How did you get on at the dentist?' she asked, as they trod carefully between the squashed fruit and empty boxes littering the market place.

'Fine,' Adrian said. 'Nothing done.'

'Good,' she said, stopping suddenly in front of a display of strawberries. 'Let's have some, shall we? Our first lot.'

Adrian imagined being back at home with his family: sitting in the dining room in front of a huge bowl of strawberries and cream, feeling the warm evening air through the open window and hearing the hiss and click of the garden sprinkler out on the lawn. Summer had always been like that. He watched his mother hand over her money and take two large punnets from the stall-keeper. There was nothing else to think about, just then: no election, no eighteen-point lead, no four more years to wait for anything. Even Mick, with his hard, tanned body and bright smile, was temporarily forgotten.

Merrick is Missing

Peter is not who he says he is. Greg knows this but he hasn't let on – and, of course, he can't now without looking stupid or causing trouble. He's known since the moment he turned the stairs in the old mews house – with its fresh magnolia paint and its single, bare light bulb – and found Merrick waiting by the open door.

Of course, if Peter had included a photo in his reply to Greg's ad, the problem would never have arisen. But the brief, hastily written note had contained just the right amount of information to make the reader want to know more, photo or no photo. Apart from which, only four other people had replied, and one of *them* lived on the Isle of Lewis.

At that first moment, on the brightly-lit, bare-walled landing, Greg was going to say: 'Well, London's a small town,' or something equally fatuous to break the ice; then the two men could have shaken their heads and smiled ironically at coincidence. But it hadn't been like that. Without a flicker of recognition on his angular face, Merrick had said: 'Hi, I'm Peter. Did you find me OK?'. Greg had reached the top of the stairs and smiled and said: 'Yeah, I found it easy.' And then it was too late.

Greg's in his bathroom, preparing for their third meeting. He's had a bath and washed his hair and now he's standing in front of the steamed-up mirror, getting ready to shave. There are two wet blobs of cotton wool on the rim of the bath, both of them twisted up into yellow points. He hasn't forgotten the first time, lying awkwardly on Peter's three-seater, and the way Peter wiggled his tongue into Greg's ear. The noise in his head was like the sound of a seashell. . .

He's been getting ready for over an hour. Two phone calls have disturbed his preparations: one from Terry, the blond computer programmer, wondering if they could meet up again; the other from Mick the Underground, wondering the same thing. The message to both is the same: 'Yeah, I'd like to see you again, but I'm really tied up with work at the moment. It looks like we'll be working overtime for a few weeks yet. Can I phone you when. . .' etc. No one can accuse Greg of being a coward – after all, he sent the man from the Isle of Lewis a postcard of a pink-haired punk standing outside Buckingham Palace. He thanked the man for replying and hoped he'd drop in if ever he were passing. A quick look in his *Reader's Digest* road atlas of the British Isles had convinced Greg that it was safe to include his address on the card.

Peter is not so easily dealt with and Greg stands in front of the bathroom mirror contemplating the dilemma. Who, he wonders, is guilty of the greater deception: Merrick Wallace, for pretending to be someone else in front of a man he believes to be a stranger, or Greg, for knowing the truth and saying nothing at the beginning? The more he's thought about it since their first meeting – and particularly since Peter's unexpected call suggesting a second – the more dishonest Greg has felt about the whole thing. Now they're on their third date in as many weeks. The shaving brush is lathered up and the razor has a new blade. Greg stands very still and draws a line in the condensation on the mirror where his mouth is; then dots for his nose and eyes. The marks begin to cloud over almost immediately but not before he's caught a glimpse of a guilty face frowning back at him across the steaming washbasin.

Saturday morning. Greg has been busy shopping for self-assembly bookshelves and matt black wall tiles for the bathroom. He meets his old friend Mark for coffee at the Out and About bar in Soho. The bar is very crowded.

'I'm sorry I'm late,' Greg says, manoeuvring himself and his various bags and boxes through the crowded café.

Mark is sitting with an empty coffee cup on the table in front of him, reading *The Daily Telegraph*.

'It's all right,' Mark says. 'I've been cruising the dispatch rider by the stairs.'

Greg tries to jam as much of his baggage under the table as he can. 'I noticed his calves when I came down the stairs. Do you want some more coffee?'

'In a minute.'

'You'll never catch a cycle dispatch rider if you read *The Telegraph* in public,' Greg says, sitting down.

'I always read it here on a Saturday morning. It shocks people.'

They chat about nothing in particular. Mark looks tired and keeps glancing across towards the stairs. After about half an hour, Greg says (because he knows Mark gets around), 'D'you know Merrick Wallace?'

Mark looks surprised. 'Yeah, sort of. Everyone knows Merrick. He's been around for years. Why?'

'Oh,' Greg says. 'I saw him last week. I hadn't seen him since I was working behind the bar at The Mitre. He used to go in there with Phil and Charlie and that crowd.'

'Oh yeah. Merrick's been around for years,' Mark says again. 'Wallace isn't his real name, you know.' Greg looked up quickly. 'It's Walenkovitz. His parents were Polish refugees from the last war. I think he changed his name by deed poll.'

Greg does a quick bit of mental arithmetic and frowns. The dispatch rider gets up and disappears up the stairs. 'Shit!' Mark says. 'There's *another* message for the classifieds.'

'Merrick's quite handsome, isn't he?'

'Yes, he is,' Mark says. 'I think I had sex with him once, years ago. I *think* it was him. . .'

'Well, *I* think he's quite handsome.'

'He looks great for his age,' Mark says. 'So didn't you speak when you saw him last week?'

Greg laughs. 'He didn't seem to recognise me from The Mitre, so I can't have made much of an impression on him back then.'

'There wouldn't have been any harm in trying,' Mark says. 'That's the trouble with you – you let life come to you instead of going out and finding it. Mind you, Merrick's a bit strange, apparently.'

'What do you mean, strange?'

'They say he's all right the first couple of times, then he goes all moody and difficult. Everyone says so. Still, from what I can remember, he was good.'

'Yeah?'

'Good with his *tongue*, I certainly remember that.' A grin creeps slowly across Mark's face. He seems to have forgotten all about the dispatch rider. 'That's assuming it *was* him.'

'Oh, it probably was,' Greg says.

Greg stands on the doorstep. The door ahead of him is new but made to look old. There are nails studded down the centre of each panel and a small window at head height with panes of swirled glass and a rough wrought-iron grille. A smudge of yellow light through the thick glass indicates that the landing light is on already. He stands for a few moments in the chilly autumn evening, trying to detect any sound from the upper rooms. The light is burning and the blinds are drawn; he expects to hear the beat of music from Peter's compact disc player, but there's no noise from the building. All he can hear is the sound of traffic passing through the square at the end of the mews and a car alarm wailing in a nearby street.

Merrick isn't the first person Greg's met who's pretending to be someone else. The men of forty who claimed to be thirty-three; the boys of seventeen who swore blind they were twenty-one; the exotic, tragic, exciting stories of a hundred and more implausible pasts – Greg's heard so many over dinner tables and under duvet covers through the last decade. It's the kind of romance he deals with best; he hasn't taken honesty for granted for a long time. But there's something different about this one.

Peter is waiting at the top of the stairs again. He's wearing faded old jeans, a purple baseball shirt with a white collar and white baseball boots. His hair is greased back off his forehead into a quiff. He smiles at Greg and kisses him on the mouth before they go into the flat, and Greg thinks: *'Well, he's still keen'*.

There's a big pile of clothes on the living-room floor and a couple of bodybuilding magazines on the arm of the sofa.

'I started the ironing,' Peter says, sweeping the clothes into a great heap against the wall. 'I haven't been working today, so I did the laundry.'

Greg can't remember if he's already risked asking Peter what he does for a living. He decides not to try it now.

'Have you been here all day?' he asks.

'No,' Peter says. 'I've been out here and there, you know. Things to do – business, mostly. . .' Greg nods.

Peter goes into the kitchen to make some tea and Greg sits on the sofa flicking through the bodybuilding magazines. The men are tanned and square-looking, like they've been filled under the skin with fibre glass. When Peter comes back, he laughs and says: 'They're too much, aren't they?' They both agree they'd like to look like that.

'I wish I'd started when I was seventeen,' Peter says, and Greg thinks: *It would serve him right if I asked how old he is.*

They're both very hungry, but there's the whole evening free. Peter puts a Kate Bush album on the CD player and crawls across the floor. He rests his arms on Greg's knees and closes his eyes for a few moments. Greg can't tell if he's unhappy or just listening to the music. Then, after a few moments, he opens his eyes and smiles. 'I thought we'd go to a restaurant I know in West Hampstead,' he says. 'We can go in the car.'

Greg looks round the room. There are cardboard boxes against the wall and a packing case just inside the kitchen door. 'How long have you been here?'

'Nine months,' Peter says. 'I know it looks as if I just moved in. I haven't had time to unpack everything, and I've got to get rid of a lot of stuff. We had a much bigger place in Highgate. Anyway, I'm not sure I really want to stay. . .'

'It's very quiet,' Greg says. 'And very central.' He thinks: *It would serve him right if I asked about his ex-lover.*

'Yeah.' Peter doesn't sound very enthusiastic. He moves forward and runs his hands across Greg's forearms. 'It's good to see you again.' Greg smiles. He feels suddenly uncomfortable, but he says, 'Yeah, and you,' and he thinks he means it.

It's raining hard outside. They run across the glistening cobbles to the car. When Peter turns the ignition key, the car phone squeaks like a small animal between them. Peter puts a cassette on and they drive out of the mews.

The rain streams across the windows, reducing the buildings and cars along Lisson Grove to smudges of trickling light. Peter says he's known the owner of the restaurant for years. Greg thinks this is strange, but he says nothing. Just before they reach West Hampstead, Peter apologises for the cassette. 'I bought the smoochy tape by mistake,' he says.

They slow down in front of a small Italian restaurant half-way along West End Lane and Peter leans forward to look past Greg. Two men are sitting at the table in the window. Behind them, the restaurant looks almost empty. One of the men looks away from his companion and stares through the window at the car.

'No,' Peter says, accelerating suddenly. 'No, we can't go there. There's someone I don't want to see.'

'Fair enough,' Greg says. Peter's looking embarrassed.

'We'll try a place in Camden I know,' he says. 'I'm sorry about this scenic tour.'

So they drive through the rain. They don't talk much, but the tape plays on. In the back of his mind, Greg half expects the car phone to ring before they reach Camden. It doesn't.

They're greeted at the door by a waitress with bright red lipstick and masses of black hair teased up high on the top of her head.

'Hi,' she says, smiling at them. And then she says to Peter: 'Haven't seen *you* for a while.'

'No, I've been busy lately. . .'

'There's a table through the back.'

The restaurant spreads through two arches under a railway viaduct. It's very crowded. When Greg looks up he notices that the ceiling, high above them, is made of corrugated iron. The waitress shows them to a table in a small brick alcove and hands them a couple of menus. Greg orders a large bottle of mineral water.

'I eat out too much,' Peter says. 'I hardly ever cook for myself at home. It's just a habit I've got into.'

Conversation takes them through to the middle of the second course. Later on, remembering their evenings together, Greg wonders what they talked about. When he counts up the number of subjects that couldn't be discussed, he's amazed to realise that they spent three evenings together with hardly a silent moment. It can't *all* have been lies. Greg is just mopping up his goulash gravy with a piece of bread when Peter says, out of the blue: 'There's something I want to tell you.'

Greg stops turning his bread round the plate and looks up. Peter's face looks hollow and pale in the candle-light, but his eyes are shining.

'Oh?' Greg pours them both another glass of mineral water. He wonders how Peter will make his confession. The way his hand shakes slightly as he reaches for his glass suggests hesitant contrition. His eyes, though, are shining with what looks like confidence. Greg has only a split second to consider his own inevitable admission.

'The thing is, I need your help.'

'Oh!'

Peter misinterprets Greg's look of surprise. 'I know. It sounds a bit dramatic, doesn't it? It's not really. In fact, it's very simple.'

'Is it?' Greg takes a long drink of mineral water and hiccups loudly.

'You've helped me already,' Peter says. 'Though I don't suppose you realised it.'

'Well, I can't say I did. . .'

Peter leans forward slightly. 'The thing is,' he says, 'I want to disappear.'

'Disappear. . .'

'I'm tired of my life the way it is. I want something new.'

Greg nods, more at the candle than at Peter. 'Yeah. . . Well I can appreciate that,' he says. 'I feel that way myself sometimes.'

'I knew you did,' Greg says. 'The first evening we met, I knew you'd help me.'

'Oh, hold on. . .' Greg begins. This is not what he expected at all.

'It's all right,' Peter says. 'Like I say, you've helped me already. I'm not going to ask you to do anything illegal or dodgy. In fact, I'm not going to ask you to do more than you've done already.'

'But what have I done?' Greg asks. Peter doesn't reply, but Greg has the beginnings of an answer at the back of his mind. 'When you say *disappear*, what do you mean exactly?'

'I mean completely, simply disappear,' Peter says, waving his hand like a conjurer. 'Go somewhere else, start a new life, be someone else.'

'Have a new name?' Greg adds, before he can stop himself.

'Naturally.'

'It's not easy to do,' Greg says. 'I mean, in practical terms. There are too many records on us. You'd have to go a long way – another country, even.'

Peter smiles. 'Oh, I'm taking that for granted. I'm sorting the practical side out slowly – one thing at a time. But that's partly why I want to do it. Doesn't it make you angry knowing you can't do what you want – be who you want?'

'Well, yeah. . .' Greg says. 'But it's partly up to you, isn't it? If you want to change, it's up to you.'

Peter shakes his head. 'It doesn't matter how much you want to change,' he says. 'If you stay in the same place, surrounded by the same things and the same people, they'll never let you be anyone else.'

'And you're tired of the same people and the same things?'

'Yes, I am.'

'Well, it makes sense,' Greg says.

The waitress comes by and collects their plates. 'Pudding?' Peter asks for the menu.

'But it's a bit hard on your friends, isn't it?' Greg continues. 'They'd be worried if you just vanished.'

'I've thought about it,' Peter says. 'For a while they would be, but they'd adapt. You can adapt to anything. Some of my friends have gone. At the time you think life'll never be the same again. I'm still sorry, but life hasn't really changed. It doesn't stop you losing your temper when the washing machine breaks down or the signals fail on the Northern Line and you know you're going to be an hour late getting somewhere. It probably should do, but it doesn't. That's what I'm tired of. If I stayed, nothing would ever change.'

'My friends are starting to die too,' Greg says.

The waitress returns. 'What's it to be, then? Death By Chocolate? Moccha Bombe?'

'Just coffee for me,' Peter says.

'And me, thanks.'

'You're unusual,' Peter says, unexpectedly. 'You're very unpushy. I noticed that straight away. I knew you'd understand what I meant when I told you.'

Greg feels awkward. 'People have a right to be private,' he says, staring into the candlelight again. 'I've always thought that. You shouldn't have to explain everything.' When he thinks about what he's just said, he feels a bit sick, as if he's just eaten Death by Chocolate.

'But you do if you have a lover,' Peter says. 'It's like an *obligation* with a lover.'

Back at the flat, Greg follows Peter into the kitchen. There's an electricity bill lying open on the table. The name is clearly visible: Merrick Wallace.

'Tea or coffee?' Peter asks.

'Tea please.'

Peter plugs in the kettle. Then he walks over to Greg, who's standing in the doorway, and puts his arms round his neck. 'I'm tired.'

'Me too.'

They take their tea into the living room and Peter puts a soul record on the CD player.

'What will you do with all your stuff?' Greg asks him. 'What'll happen to this place? What about money? How are you going to arrange that?'

'The flat's for sale,' Peter says. 'I haven't got a board up because I don't want my friends to know. Someone's already made an offer. I'm just waiting to hear. I'll sell all the things I can't take with me. None of it's rubbish.'

'I can see that,' Greg says, looking round the room.

'Money's a bit difficult to sort out, but I'll manage it. I'll just lock the door behind me and go.'

'But it can't be that easy. . .'

Peter laughs. 'Oh, it isn't *easy*. . .'

They go to bed and fall asleep to the sound of rain hitting the window and the low hum of the fridge-freezer in the kitchen.

The next morning, the sun's shining on the cobbles in the mews. Greg presses his nose against the window and the glass feels cold. It's Sunday morning and all the curtains in the houses across the mews are drawn tight.

'I ought to be going,' he says. 'I've got things to do at home.'

'Well, if you're sure.' Peter is under the duvet, his head propped up against two pillows, drinking a mug of tea. 'I don't usually go out early on Sunday, but I promised my friends I'd be in Brighton by eleven thirty. You're welcome to stay in bed and let yourself out.'

'No, really,' Greg says. 'I've got a lot to do.' He's thinking about the electricity bill on the kitchen table.

They leave the flat together. Peter drives Greg to the nearest tube station. Before he gets out of the car, Greg says: 'Have a good time in Brighton.'

Peter smiles. 'Take care.'

'Talk to you soon.' And then Greg gets out of the car. The air is cold against his face. People walk past, newspapers heaped in their arms. He looks back and waves. Peter is still smiling. He waves back and drives away.

The following Saturday evening, Greg goes to his old flatmates' party. Sarah and Keith are both qualified solicitors now and live in a flat with stripped floorboards near Battersea Park. There are lots of people Greg has never met before and a few familiar faces from the old days. None of their clothes seem to fit or hang properly. Kate Bush is played a lot on the CD player.

Greg has been there two hours when he passes one of the bedroom doors and hears Sarah talking to one of their friends. 'I spoke to Greg,' she says. 'He seems well.'

'It's hard to *tell*, though, isn't it?' the other girl says. 'I must have chatted to him for about twenty minutes; and when he'd gone I realised he hadn't told me anything – nothing about what *he's* been doing.'

'Well, you know Greg,' Sarah says. 'He's never given much away.'

'But it's like he can't be bothered sometimes.'

'I do love him,' Sarah says. 'I worry about him. Keith does, too. I just wish he'd meet someone nice. It's so risky being casual these days. He deserves someone nice.'

'Maybe we ought to keep an eye on him,' the other girl says. 'Make sure he's all right.'

'Yes, that's probably a good idea,' Sarah says. 'How are things with Shaun?'

'Oh God, they're so much *better* these days! I feel like I'm really getting through to him at last.'

Greg hurries into the bathroom. He pulls his jacket out from under the coats and scarves piled high on the laundry basket. Then he tiptoes along the hall, past the living room where Ella Fitzgerald is singing the blues, and slips, unnoticed, out of the flat.

Another month passes. Greg paints his living room pale blue and fixes the tiles on the bathroom wall. The man from the Isle of Lewis sends a postcard with a picture of a highland pony on the front. He says he's always wanted to visit London and may come down before the winter sets in. Is there any chance of him staying with Greg for a few nights?

One Friday night, Greg gets ready to go out to the local bar. It's ten o'clock and he's sitting at the living-room table trying to compose a draft letter to the man from Lewis, when the telephone rings.

'Surprise,' a voice says.

'Hello,' Greg says. 'How are you?'

'I'm all right,' Peter says. 'Are you surprised to hear from me?'

'I am a bit – I thought you must have gone.'

'I don't know if you've tried to phone me,' Peter says. 'Only I've been out a lot.'

'Oh.'

'I've been waiting to sell the flat. It's all settled now.'

'So you're ready to go?' Greg says.

'Well, almost. How've you been keeping?'

'Very well, thanks. And you?'

'Fine.' There's a slight pause and then Peter says: 'I've been thinking about you. You know, some people might say you were difficult. . .'

'Might they?' Greg asks, surprised.

'I don't really know much about you,' Peter says.

'You never asked much about me.'

'I know.'

'What I did say was the truth. . .'

There isn't even a second's pause on the other end of the phone.

'I'm still going,' Peter says. 'Only I've been holding on a while.'

'Why?'

Greg hears a half-concealed cough.

'I was. . .'

'Yeah?'

'I've been wondering if you'd be prepared to come with me. I know it's crazy. . .'

Greg really *is* confused.